He looked at her long and sighed, "You know, Satin, you should probably stay away from me."

"Yes, I know," she answered, "but I don't know that I can. Do you wish me to?"

He flicked her nose and then suddenly he was pulling her to the side of the building, hiding her from view, pushing her gently against the Inn's outer wall, for he felt himself out of control. "No, Satin, I want you in my way, but I make you no promises beyond this." He was bending down, touching her lips with his own.

Hers parted to receive his kiss, and her hands went to his shoulder. She moved into his arms and he held her tightly as one kiss moved into another, and she heard his voice, low, seductive, and so very enticing; "I want you, Satin. . . ."

LORD WILDFIRE

CLAUDETTE WILLIAMS

FAWCETT CREST • NEW YORK

Chapter One

Lady Satin curled a short, thick tress of black hair round her slender finger and bit her full lower lip. A tear formed in one dark eye, but she held it back. She wouldn't cry. No one, not even her father, was going to make her cry. She stood against his tirade and allowed him to finish.

"And it is no use standing there looking for all the world like an innocent kitten, for we know that you are not! Don't we?"

"I have never claimed to be innocent and I am certainly not a kitten," she answered in what she hoped was a meek tone.

It wasn't, and she had only fueled his temper higher. "No, certes, you would rather think yourself a tigress, ready to take on the jungle! Well, by God, you are not such a creature but you have taken on the jungle and will be slaughtered!" He shook his head. "That you could have gone behind my back, without my knowledge, against my expressed wishes . . ."

"Papa, I used a pseudonym. No one will ever find out the true identity of the author. I have Mr. Murry's word on it."

"Ha! What do we know of Murry? Who is to say he won't reveal your name for a price?"

"He won't. Besides, Byron publishes through him and Byron said he is to be trusted."

Her father nearly had a convulsion. "*Byron?* I don't trust *Byron*! And that is another thing! I won't have you in Byron's pocket. The man is a libertine. Why, it is rumored that he and his sister . . ."

"Papa! Byron is my friend." Satin blushed an attractive shade of pink. "I won't gossip about him. The subject here is my novel and how well my secret may be kept. It will be."

"Byron brought Lady Caroline low . . . ruined her," her father persisted.

"No, Lady Caro ruined herself with her public displays," was his daughter's grave response. "Papa, we needed the money Mr. Murry was kind enough to advance me for my book . . ."

"And *I* would have found the money," he answered sharply, displeased that she had reminded him that he had not handled their funds quite sanely after his wife's death. Some years had passed since Satin's mother had died, and he didn't seem to be able to get a hold of his finances.

"Of course, Papa," she answered immediately. "However, the sum I was advanced was only to allow you some time . . . so that whatever investments you make, you may do at your own pace." She shrugged her shoulders. "My book will probably only sell in a moderate quantity, and no one will even raise a brow over the author's name. After all, Felix Gamble sounds like an adventurer or a cit, but not," she teased in mock dismay, "a noble lady."

He frowned, still displeased and ill at ease over the business.

"Nevertheless . . ."

Their housekeeper, Maudly, appeared at the library door after having opened it a fraction. "Count Otto Stauffenberg is here to see Lady Satin."

Waverly was an old name, but theirs was an impoverished estate and the earl's hope was to marry his daughter, Satin, to a wealthy peer. The count was a favored swain, and though Satin had him ever by her side, she did not seem inclined to bring matters to a point.

To his daughter, he said quickly under his breath, "We will discuss this later." Then to his housekeeper, "Show the count in at once."

The German count was a tall and largely built man. His years numbered some two and thirty; his hair was dark and lightly laced with gray. His eyes were a soft brown, his face merry and his full lips shaded by the thickness of his dark moustache. He was a dashing figure of a man who had suffered through an early marriage that had left him widowed and quite rich.

"There you are," he said in his thick German accent, the smile already wide across his round face. "We will be late, you know."

She laughed. "Now, is that my fault? I have been here awaiting you, sir!"

"Well, where is your spencer then? Go on . . . get your bonnet, too, while I chat with your father."

She bobbed him a curtsy and hurried off. What she would do without the count stalling her father's insistence on her choosing a husband she did not know. She was already one and twenty, and her father was determined to see her married. She and Otto were friends, and thus far, he seemed content to keep it that way. He announced himself to the world as her devoted servant, but made no push towards that end in private.

Some minutes later she reentered the library to discover Otto chatting away with her father, who was growing more red-faced by the moment. "That's right," Otto was saying, "they say it has sold five thousand copies already. Everyone is talking about it. I want to pick a copy up on the way to the fairgrounds today. They say . . ." He saw Satin and stopped. "Have you heard about it, Satin?"

"Heard? About what, Otto?" She held her breath, hoping that she was wrong and at the same time discovering that her heart was beating wildly over the possibility that it was actually her novel that had sold so many copies.

"That new book, *Passion's Seed,*" he returned in a tone of excited expectancy.

"Nooo . . ." she answered hesitantly. Faith! What was she going to do? This was beyond her hopes. A fearsome thing, and yet so very satisfying. She couldn't tell anyone. "What about it?" she pursued, keeping her eyes from glancing towards her father.

"I am told that the author—whom no one seems to know—knows everything about the haut ton. Everything we have done for the last four . . . maybe three seasons . . . is described in what Lady Hester tells me is fine style. She says Lord Butterworth, though he is called Butterball in the book, had her convulsed in giggles . . ."

"But isn't it fiction?" Lady Satin's dark eyes opened wide. She never dreamed that anyone would recognize themselves. She had written it for the growing English middle class, not for the beau monde's notice.

"Oh, the author changed the names, but fiction?" He laughed and shook his head. "Not according to what I have heard. Come, we will stop and pick up a copy."

She took up her white spencer and its matching white straw bonnet, plopping it on top of her short, black curls and allowing Otto to stop her a moment to set the bonnet correctly. With his critical eye he looked her over. She was an alluring piece of fluff, but what caught his attention was the fire in her dark eyes and the sassiness of her smile. With a sound of approval he bent and offered his arm, but she stalled him a moment and turned to her father.

"Till later then, Papa?"

Otto added quickly, "Don't worry, my lord, I will take care of your Lady Satin."

"How you will manage that is beyond me, for I tell you frankly I have never been able to handle that particular chore!" her father returned with a rueful smile.

"Oh, Papa!" the lady objected.

"Go on then, go on." He waved them off and then watched as the door closed at their backs. What to do? Here was a muddle, indeed. The Earl of Waverly put a hand to his forehead and sank into his worn, leather wing chair. He scanned his desk. Just how would he manipulate his daughter in this situation? There was bound to be trouble, perhaps scandal of the worst kind. Her book had sold already five thousand copies. Out less than a week and already sought after by the fashionable members of their own class! The beau monde would forgive one of their own many things, but this?

Just how would they see this latest escapade of Satin's? As a betrayal! How else could they see it? As a member of the highest aristocratic set, Satin was privy to the confidences of all sorts. Using such things, even in so-called fiction . . . ? The horror of it boggled the earl's mind. She was his only child, his treasure. She was all that was left to him of his late wife, and somehow he saw this escapade as his fault. If Satin had not been out to take care of his debts, she would not have written and sold that miserable piece of scribbling!

He groaned. Satin, with her sense of humor, had taken on the beau monde full score and had put down their antics, their indiscretions, their foibles, weaving the facts into a tale of pure mirth and romance. Hero and heroine might be fictional characters, but few others were. What to do? What would Lady Jersey do? They would oust Satin from Almack's . . . from London! Egad! Look what they did to Lady Caroline. Caroline had written such a novel and she had been banished, shamed, belittled by all those who mattered to the earl. He couldn't, wouldn't, allow his daughter to suffer such a fate.

Certes! What to do? If ever there was a muddle of

Satin's doing, here it was. She was his naughty girl, his daring puss, his impulsive rough-and-tumble prize. How to save her? There was, of course, his sister Jane. Ye gods! That he should have to resort to this. Jane.

With a long and somewhat worn sigh, he took up a quill and started his letter. So, just as she had predicted, he was again applying to her for assistance. Lady Jane was a formidable figure whose presence in his household would most certainly cut up his peace, but there was no other way.

She resided for most of the year in her late husband's ancestral home in the wilds of Romney Marsh. He had always thought that odd and at variance with her town-styled nature, but then there was never any saying what Jane would and would not take to. So there she was, out in that drafty, old castle, wielding her power over the fashionables (and he doubted there even were any) in the small, quaint town of Rye. Did her power with the haut ton still extend itself to London's beau monde? Aye. He was fairly certain that it did. So then here was his ticket to safety for his daughter and himself. Lady Jane. He would send for her, and she would be certain to come. Theirs were different natures. She took after their father and he after their mother, but they had a common bond and that was their affection for Satin.

Ah, Satin, miserable girl, do you know what your father sacrifices for you? he asked silently as he signed his name to the letter.

Indeed, Satin would have been very much surprised to find that her father was moved to such drastic measures. In spite of the fact that she was watching the count purchase a copy of her novel from a stack of neatly and prominently displayed copies of *Passion's Seed*, she still felt she was in no danger of discovery. After all, how would anyone make the

connection between the male name she had chosen
to use and herself?

She did, however, experience a ripple of excitement as she watched Otto flip through the pages of
this, her first book. My word, she thought to herself,
people are actually paying money to read something
I composed! It was quite a feeling.

"Here," Otto said, pushing the book into her
hands without further ado and putting a halt to her
wandering thoughts. "You will skim through it
while we take the ride to the fairgrounds and tell me
if it is worth my attention."

"Ha!" she returned, giving his arm a playful rap.
"Beast. Always trying to put me to work. Why
should I do that? You read it for yourself, sir." She
thrust the packaged novel back at him, but before he
could argue, a voice at her back called their attention.

"Lady Satin . . ." It was a distinctive male drawl,
and although the address of the man was decidely
languid, there was a certain masculinity that caught
and held the interest.

Satin's dark eyes opened wide and the woman in
her lit their depths. She gave the gentleman a soft
smile as she put out her gloved hand in genuine pleasure. Sir Edward Danton bent over it, but instead of
kissing the gloved fingers, he easily, deftly found the
uncovered wrist, and his lips lingered audaciously.
His hazel eyes moved and met her own dark orbs,
and he was satisfied when he felt her tremble.

Indeed, Satin trembled, though it was unlike her.
She had some experience in handling the London
rakes and her style was simple but always effective.
She would return their flirtation, but she always
kept on the move and never gave an answer that
could come back to haunt her. Most of the libertines
took her responses in the light nature they were intended, for she was quality and the general rule was
not to dive too deeply with their own set. That would

end in marriage, and a rake avoided that state at all costs.

Sir Edward, however, was different. For one thing, he was *not* considered a rake. He was not even counted amongst those in the petticoat line. Sir Edward was, in fact, something of a dandy. His chestnut curls were lightly pomaded and framed his lean, attractive face. His brows were finely shaped over his light hazel eyes. His lips were thin, his dress exquisite. His conversation was witty, fluent and interesting. No invitation list was complete without his name. He was considered the best of good ton and his wealth and lineage made him a prize on the marriage mart. He broke the hearts of mamas though, for up until now he had never displayed an interest in the misses presented during the season.

He made Lady Satin move closer, for he did not immediately release her hand; instead, easily, indiscernibly, he brought her to him and his drawl lowered to a soft, husky tone. "Your obedient servant, my lady." He turned to smile sweetly at the count, who was by now pulling a face. "My dear count, one wonders how it is you manage, in spite of that deplorable habit you have of donning a gray greatcoat, to wield Lady Satin on your arm."

The large count started to bluster out a reply, but Satin put a restraining hand on his upper arm and said lightly, "La, Sir Edward, the color suits him, don't you think?"

"What is the matter with gray?" the count demanded.

"It is Napoleon's color," Sir Edward drawled, his sneer marked. "As nearly everyone knows, but then, I have heard your views lean in that direction. . . ."

It was a bait, just the sort of bait to set two men against one another, for Napoleon and Wellington were in the very heat of battle in Spain and there were sects of Napoleon sympathizers in England.

"Politics!" Satin stood between the two men and

stamped her foot. "It's not a subject open to discussion in a Bond Street book shop!" She lifted her piquant face to the count's. "Now, as I recall, you promised me a trip to the fair."

"Very neat," Sir Edward whispered in her ear. "My felicitations, you handle him well."

To this, Satin frowned, and, pulling Otto who made no secret of his feelings about this encounter, she managed to get out of the shop. "Oh, stop . . ." She laughed as Otto handed her into his closed carriage and climbed in after her. "I don't know why you allow him to annoy you . . . why, it only makes him do it all the more."

"He wants you," Otto pronounced after a moment's silence.

"Does he?" she said, surprised. "I don't think so."

"You are naive," the count returned. "I have never seen him attend to any marriageable chit before . . . yet he seems, more and more, to seek you out and pay you considerable notice."

"You are mistaken," she answered. "Sir Edward is not interested in me. Why, I have been out two seasons, so why should he suddenly decide to have me in my third season? It doesn't make sense."

Otto frowned. "Just a moment, my girl. Sir Edward was in Greece when you were first presented two years ago, and he doesn't hunt, so he was not with us when we all went up to the riding country and the Quorn."

"Yes, but he was introduced to me last spring," she said thoughtfully, "and I can't remember his showing any signs of succumbing to my many charms last season." She batted her eyelashes at him playfully.

"Minx!" Otto laughed and tweaked her nose. "It took him some time, perhaps, but I think he has succumbed; mark me, my girl, he wants you." Then he went serious again. "And I think you rather like him."

"He is ever so attractive, Otto." She sighed.

"He is dangerous." The count shook his head. "He is not for you."

"Do you think he will break my heart?" she asked curiously.

"No, but he won't make you happy. He is too cold inside . . . about too much, and Satin . . . you are too gay. You need someone who may curb you, not tame you."

"And who may that be, Otto?" she queried.

He sighed. "God only knows!"

Sir Edward stepped outside and watched the count's carriage being driven off into London's hubbub of traffic. A flower girl waved a daffodil at him.

"Fer yer loidy, sir . . . a ha'penny will do . . ." It was very nearly a plea.

He eyed her a moment. She was dressed in an ensemble of ill-fitting and mismatched pieces of clothing; her hair might have been a fair shade beneath the soot and grime, and she appeared a good deal older than the twelve years she numbered. He thought of Satin and found himself reaching into his pocket and flipping the child a coin. A moment later he was asking himself what in the hell he was doing. He refused the flower, took up his ebony walking stick and proceeded down the avenue. He was irritated beyond belief. What was happening to him? He wanted Satin to the point of distraction. He even found himself doing a thing because something in the back of his mind told him that Satin would like it. Well, this was going to have to stop!

In the past he had allowed courtesans to take care of his needs and it had always served, but from the moment he had met Lady Satin he had discovered a new side to himself and it was most agitating! Satin? She aroused sensations in his breast he hadn't been aware he was capable of feeling any longer. Satin? She didn't seem adverse to his attentions, yet she didn't seem to encourage him to further them either. She seemed perfectly content to allow that dolt to squire her everywhere!

Satin. She was not quite in his usual style. He had always favored tall, elegant ladies who were sophisticated and worldly. Satin was as much child as she was woman. She was full of impulse, spirit and something he could not name, and while she was certainly adorable in her youthful beauty, he had known many beautiful women in his time. Why then did she occupy all his thoughts?

Well, there was nothing for it. He had admitted to himself some days ago that he had to have her and damn it all to hell, one way or another, Sir Edward meant to have her; so he set himself to discovering all he could about her. Ah, the lady enjoyed writing. A slip she made to him once about an article she had published when she was away at school got him to thinking. Then there was her friendship with Byron, the poet, and Murry, the publisher. He wasn't sure when it came to his head that there was something about this new book, *Passion's Seed,* that disturbed him, but disturb him it did. So he took it up and read it, and before long, he was reading it again.

Chapter Two

The ninth duke of Morland's black, gleaming coach was stopped in the heat of London's busy traffic. Hawkers cried out their wares and looked hopefully towards the impressive coach. One young and incredibly dirty boy sidled up to the duke's coach and stuck an apple through its window.

"Bright 'n shiny it be . . . jest right fer ye, guvnor." He grinned and displayed a mouth devoid of teeth.

" 'Ere . . . shuv off—" the duke's postilion started to shout at the urchin.

The duke tapped at his driver's box and stuck his head out the window. "Never mind, Harly . . ." He smiled at the boy and flipped him a coin. He was rewarded with the apple and the boy's parting thanks as the lad ran back into the hubbub of the traffic to try his luck again.

The duke turned to his companion and handed him the apple. "Just the thing to keep you quiet," his grace said, his bright, Irish blue eyes twinkling.

Sir Charles Liverpool looked at the fruit with some contempt and set it aside. "I won't be put off, Nick. It is time you reentered society. It's been more than five months since your father's death, five months since you left the Peninsula and . . ."

"And I am in mourning," the duke replied, cutting his cousin off with what he hoped was an end to the discussion.

"Don't pitch your gammon at me. We both loved

your father; damnation, Nick, he was more a father to me than my own was, but he would not have wanted you to bury yourself in the wilds and forget what life has to offer!"

"No, and I haven't exactly done that, now have I?" returned the duke with something of a grin.

"I wouldn't call living up in your hunting box and running the countryside ragged with those hounds of yours . . ."

"And what of the excellent . . . er . . . dinners we had afterwards this winter? Wasn't that putting aside our mourning?" his grace shot back, this time definitely grinning.

Sir Charles paused. They had, in fact, brought into the hunting box some very fine fancy pieces and together with their cronies, they had indeed managed to enjoy themselves. He frowned. "Don't evade the issue. That is not what I am talking about."

The duke tipped his dark beaver top hat over his eyes, sank into his leather-upholstered squabs, folded his arms across his chest and sighed. "Do stubble it, my dear Charles, for you weary me."

"Weary you? Well, and so I shall until you agree to go into society again and give some thought to . . . to . . . carrying on the name."

"What the devil for? I have you to do that for me."

"Me? I don't carry the name . . . and besides, I haven't met . . . well, I'm not ready to . . . Look here, we are not talking about me. We are talking about—"

"Me!" the duke exclaimed, shaking his head ruefully. "That is the trouble: we are always talking about me."

"As is everyone in London!" returned Sir Charles relentlessly. "They say 'Lord Wildfire' is so only on the battlefield and that you have lost your touch with women." Here, a bit of bait to taunt his cousin's ego.

He knew what he was doing. Lord Wildfire (a nickname the young duke had received from his men after certain victorious battles against the French) turned and eyed Sir Charles with a touch of irritation. "Now how would anyone know whether or not I have done that?" Definitely a challenge there.

They had by this time arrived in the heart of the buzzing fairgrounds, and the coach had come to a full halt. Sir Charles ignored the question and jumped nimbly down from the carriage, pointing up with his cane to the driver. "We shan't need you, old chap, for at least an hour, so do go off and enjoy yourself . . ."

The duke alighted, heard this and, as his driver looked for reassurance on the matter, nodded his head; to his cousin he said with a touch of affection, "Do feel free to order my people about as you do me . . ."

There was, however, no time for further banter, for at that precise moment something occurred that captured their entire attention.

"No, Otto, don't . . ." Lady Satin offered doubtfully, yet in spite of her concern, one could detect a gleam in her dark, impish eyes. "We will call down trouble on our heads . . ." she added as further inducement, tugging his sleeve as she spoke.

"Ha! Since when did that ever stop us?" returned her large friend, with which he climbed onto the first step of the contraption clearly inscribed for all interested individuals as a "catch-me-who-can."

Newly designed, constructed and invitingly displayed, its black, gleaming metal structure stood fenced off from the hub of the crowd. It was London's portable steam engine. A mechanical treasure advertised as "power subduing animal speed."

"Do you really think it can go faster than a horse?" Satin asked in wide-eyed wonder as Otto managed to climb still higher up. "Otto, be careful, I don't think it looks very steady."

"Faster than a horse!" he snorted. "It's too heavy . . . too clumsy . . ."

"Otto," Satin started to squeak, "Otto . . . *it's moving*!"

"Oi . . . oi say there guv'," called out the watchman who was coming back on duty from his short respite, "ye shouldn't be there. Cum on down."

However, it was at this juncture that the "catch-me-who-can" broke away with a great, creaking groan and began sliding down the avenue. As it crashed through its fencing, Satin screamed, and the watchman declared that it was the flash guv's fault as it hadn't been secured to take on anyone's weight.

"Yes, yes, of course, but do something!" Satin cried in some distress as she ran after the engine that, though moving, had not taken on any great speed. "Otto?" she called. "*Otto*, jump for mercy's sake . . . just jump off!"

Otto was looking around in some perplexity and a great deal of consternation. If he jumped, he might land hard and do himself injury. What then? He noticed the steering wheel and thought he could at least steer the miserable vehicle uphill and away from the rather massive tent he seemed to be approaching. Right then, he took hold of the wheel.

This "catch-me-who-can" was a model meant for display. Certain aspects of its design had been left unfinished. Unfortunately, one of these unfinished items was the steering wheel. It was not connected to anything in particular, and when Otto took hold of it, the thing came away nicely into his kid-gloved hands. He stood, the engine taking on speed, the wheel firmly held up in his hands, and then the tent loomed brightly before him!

Satin could see that there wasn't anything she could do, yet she ran on, unaware of anyone in her path, and found herself in the arms of a tall and perfectly attractive male specimen. However, this was not the moment to do more than notice vaguely that this was the case for he held her up (an excellent thing, as the force of their meeting could have sent them both sprawling).

"Steady," the male said in an authoritative voice.

"Oh!" said Satin, looking away to see the "catch-me-who-can" taking on the huge tent in marvelously outrageous might. She closed her eyes. "Oh, God!"

What followed next kept the crowd of spectators (of which there had gathered quite a number) in breathless awe. The tent of red, yellow and blue released an anguished groan as the steam engine plowed forcefully into the tent's central oak beam and came to a crashing halt. Screaming hysteria inside the tent took on frightful proportions as merchants and their customers began scrambling for the exit. Then with air-shattering might and in a domino effect the tent's remaining beams began to fall erratically to earth. Caught beneath the weight were silks, satins, pillows, china and various other sundries. Also caught as the heavy canvas floated heavily down were the Count Otto Stauffenberg and one outraged merchant.

People are odd beings for just when a situation will call for a calm head and clear thinking, they will, as a mob, run, cry and fitfully display their inadequacies to deal with the same. Hysteria took over, and Charles, looking from the spectacle to the crowd, turned to the duke and managed, "I say . . ."

"Otto!" Satin cried distressfully. "He is still in there!"

Sir Charles discovered that his cousin was holding in a tight grip yet another of his friends. "Certes!" he exclaimed. "If it isn't Satin! What the devil have you been up to this time, imp?"

"Chuck . . ." Satin, finding a familiar face, broke away from the duke's hold and took hold of Sir Charles's lapels. "Otto is in there. He might be hurt—and what do you mean? I haven't done a thing."

It was at this moment that Otto found a way out of the massive mess around him and he emerged, still clutching the engine's steering wheel. At his back was one irate merchant demanding just retribution for the damages, and the two were bellowing at one another.

"It would be Otto." Sir Charles shook his head with mild disgust. "How you two can kick up a lark everywhere you go, is quite beyond belief."

"Oh ho! Look who is talking," riposted Satin, one gloved hand going to her hip. "But thank goodness he is not hurt."

"Demented," answered Sir Charles, "but, no, he seems all in one piece."

"Stop it." Satin laughed. "It was an accident, after all . . ."

"They are always accidents," returned Sir Charles.

"Excuse me," said the duke in a quiet yet strangely compelling tone. "May I suggest that we escort the lady away from"— he looked around at the beadles coming their way and the returning merchants who were hot and heavy with indignation —"from all this?"

"Quite right," said Sir Charles, taking her arm.

"But, Chuck, I cannot leave Otto . . ."

"As your father would have the count's head, we would be doing him a favor by spiriting you away."

"But he doesn't know . . . Chuck . . ."

"I will signal to him. Nick, do take Lady Satin to our carriage. I will join you in a moment."

Thus it was that Lord Wildfire met Lady Satin!

Chapter Three

It wasn't until Satin had been deposited within the confines of the duke's luxurious coach that she was able to take stock of her surroundings and her companion. This she did in her easy and all-too-open manner. Her dark eyes appraised, admired and twinkled as her ruby lips formed into a sweet smile. Finding that the gentleman sitting across from her was more than just a little attractive, she became vaguely aware of her own appearance and went about the business of setting her bonnet, which had gone askew, neatly over her dark, short curls. Oddly enough, she felt a moment's awkwardness and knew she was intimidated by the man's air of self-assurance and good looks. She tried idle conversation.

"What a dreadful muddle. I can't wonder *what* you must think . . . Poor Otto . . . the Count Stauffenberg . . ." She frowned. "I really don't think I should just run off like this and leave him to his fate."

All the while the duke was thinking, what a minx! Just who was she? Pretty little thing . . . lovely body, but who the deuce was she and why had he never seen her before? He had been called Wildfire for many reasons, one of them being the speed with which he went through the ladies. His conquests on the battlefield and in the ballroom rivaled one another, to be sure.

"This Otto," he inquired gently, "a relation, no doubt?"

She giggled, covered her lips and composed herself. "No, a friend."

Aha, he thought, a beau. "He does not seem to me to be a very steady individual. What friend would bring a lady to this sort of—"

"Just a minute!" She halted him at once. "He is the best of good friends, and he brought me here because it was my wish to attend the fair . . ." She thought to add, lest he attempt to argue the point, "Besides, my father gave his permission, so there can be no question of propriety."

He had seen her dark eyes flash, and they had caught his attention. A beauty, indeed, and the duke was well able to appreciate her spirit. No demure miss this. Who the devil was she?

Sir Charles appeared at the coach door. "Well, that's done, Satin m'girl, though what Otto can be at bringing you to this place and then taking a steam engine for a ride is more than I can fathom!" He climbed in and waved off Satin's verbal objection. "Nick, I took the liberty of directing your driver to Lady Satin's town house. I hope you don't mind."

"Now why should I mind that when you have been directing my driver all morning?" There was amusement in the duke's blue eyes. "However, I hope you will find a moment to introduce me to this young lady before the journey is completed."

Sir Charles gave his cousin a quick, troubled glance. "So I shall, but not until I have warned her about you." He turned to Satin. "This gentleman is a devil, Satin m'girl, so I have my qualms about bringing him to your notice; however, there is nothing for it, so"—he inclined his head—"the Lady Satin Waverly, my cousin, his grace, the Duke of Morland."

Lady Satin was impressed, and as her full lower lip dropped just enough to entice, her gloved hand was taken up. The duke's touch was light and experienced as he found the soft flesh of her wrist and touched it with his lips. His deep blue eyes discovered her dark, penetrating glance, and he smiled to see her blush.

"Ah, I see that you are aptly named. As soft and beautiful as satin is," he said quietly.

She attempted to regain her usual composure. "Chuck, you are certainly right. He is charming enough to be dangerous, but you said *your cousin*? How have I never met him before?" She looked curiously from one to the other, for Sir Charles and Lady Satin had become fast friends early in her first season.

"Ah," said Charles, "you are not only looking at one of London's former rakehells"—he smiled and the banter was in his tone—"but also one of Wellington's heroes! He has been off fighting in the Peninsula . . ." He halted all the other questions that came flooding through Satin's mind by adding, "Here we are," as the coach pulled up to the curbing.

It was Charles who alighted and turned to give Lady Satin his gloved hand and escort her to her front door, but it was the duke who managed to stay her with a soft remark.

"This meeting ends too quickly and with no promise for the future . . ." It was a mild flirtation, but it had the power to shake Satin's calm.

Softly, she gave him an answer. "The future itself is a promise, your grace, for it is ever full of surprises." So saying, she turned and allowed Charles to take her up the walk to her father's front door. Before Maudly could appear to admit her, she turned to question Sir Charles.

"Chuck, has he sold out? And what was a duke doing in Wellington's army? That doesn't make sense. How is it he isn't married? He seems quite old enough. How old is he? Thirty . . . ?"

"Mind your manners, brat," her friend responded with a laugh. "He is not for you."

"Oh ho! And you have decided that? Well, as a matter of fact, I don't want him, but I am curious."

"He was a marquess and only recently inherited his father's title and estate. He is not married and he is old enough. Old enough and experienced enough to steal your heart off before you are even aware he wants it."

"Hmmm . . . but he isn't more than thirty . . ."

"And he is. Thirty-three to be exact and every year of it. Do you take m'meaning, girl." It was more a statement than a question.

The door opened and Maudly appeared, curtsied and ushered her charge within, but not before Lady Satin managed to throw over her shoulder, "Oh, Chuck, you do come to Southby's soirée tomorrow night?"

"Indeed, I am looking forward to it." His fine brow was up, for it appeared to his penetrating eye that Lady Satin seemed a bit more overjoyed at his answer than was called for in this instance.

"Do you bring your cousin?" she could not refrain from asking and so answered his silent question.

He was not pleased. The fact was that he was smitten with Satin and had been for two years. From the beginning he had realized that the feeling was one-sided and that she felt only friendship for him. There was balm in the knowledge that at least she was not taken with anyone else. In fact, Satin seemed immune to all.

"You will do well to remember what I am about to impart to you, my lady," he said on a frosty note. "I do not bring my cousin anywhere. He is his own man and goes where he chooses. Furthermore, he had the entrée to London's ballrooms long before you were ever out of the schoolroom!"

She stamped her foot at him, and a moment later

the door was closed and he was hopping back into the duke's waiting coach.

"I am sorry," he apologized to his cousin, "your day at the fair was ruined, and I did so want you to—to lose yourself for a bit in some harmless devilry."

The duke released a short laugh. "My dear Charles, that is precisely what I was doing." His grin was wide as he was pleased to find his cousin silenced at last.

Sir Charles closed his mouth after a moment and grunted, but he had occasion to recall the sight of Otto's escapade with the steam engine and he gave a short laugh. "Lord, but Otto is a rogue. He is forever after a lark, and one never knows what next he will be into."

This drew on his memory and the next few minutes were spent in retelling some of his wild friend's adventures on the hunting field over the last few seasons. "They are a pair, those two . . ." Charles sighed. "Good fun . . ."

"Hmmm. She appears to be something of a minx though . . . not exactly in your usual style, Charles," the duke commented interestedly.

"And what is my style?" Charles smiled.

"You do want her, don't you?" the duke pursued, ignoring his cousin's question.

"With all my heart, but, though she hasn't said so, she doesn't think we would suit," Charles answered. "She has often said we make the best of friends with the intention of, I rather think, putting off any romantic notions I might have." Charles eyed his cousin speculatively. "But may I also say that she is most definitely *not* in your style, Nick."

"You may say it . . . and as it happens, I agree with you. She is not the sort of female I intend to dally with. Since when have I ever played with virgins?"

"Just so," Charles answered and then looked at him hard, for there was the touch of the old bitterness in his voice. "She wanted to know if you meant to show yourself at Southby's tomorrow night." Now why did he tell him that?

The duke looked surprised. "And your answer?"

"I told her that you were not the man to bat her eyes at!" Charles was almost testy.

"Very good, Charles." Nick laughed.

"Well?" returned his cousin.

"Well what?" the duke answered maddeningly, enjoying himself immensely.

"Damn it, man! Do you intend to go?"

"We'll see," was all the answer he was able to give for, indeed, his mind was elsewhere as he tipped his hat to an old flame whose coach had come up alongside just at that moment.

Chapter Four

Spring touches all romantics in a way no other season can. Odes are written to it, children dance to it, lovers dream because of it. It intoxicates the imagination with its scents and sounds. So it was in the spring of 1813 at Southby's soirée in London.

Two names made headlines and gossip columns on a regular basis. Those same two names reigned over society's fribbles because of their daring and their offhanded manners; they were Lord Byron and Beau Brummell. One was a noble poet; the other a valet's son who had managed to become the Prince Regent's friend and fashion's dandy king. Satin had each at her side as the Duke of Morland came strolling into Southby's ballroom.

He saw her at once. She wore a flame-tinted gown that clung mischievously to her provocative body. Her short black curls framed her piquant face. Her dark eyes glinted with amusement as she gave Lord Byron a playful rap for some remark he had made, and then her dark eyes looked across the crowded marble floor and met a pair of deep blue eyes.

It was almost startling to discover that she was capable of feeling missish, but that was how she suddenly felt. Schoolgirl? You are not, she told herself. Quickly, she attempted to recover and inclined her head, allowing him a silent greeting.

He almost smirked as he moved towards his host and away from her. Damn! How did she manage to keep Byron and Brummell so long at her side?

Brummell did not have his habitual expression of boredom and Byron too seemed animated . . . what was this? Was she rogue or innocent?

"Nick, you devil!" It was Sir Charles coming towards him. "You gave me the distinct impression that you would not show this evening, and here you are."

The duke smiled but ignored the statement as he shook hands with Southby and made an outrageous remark to Southby's latest lady. He then followed this up by whispering into her ear. She touched him with her fan, inclined her fair head of curls and said that she didn't think Southby would mind.

"Mind?" spluttered the portly older man. "Of course I mind, you naughty piece of fluff."

She released a ripple of musical laughter and moved off towards the orchestra. Southby turned to the duke. "What's this, Wildfire, stealing me wench right out from under me nose?" Banter was in his tone.

"I am persuaded she is much too attached to you." The duke smiled and turned to find his quarry now standing with Count Stauffenberg. "She is merely . . . ah . . ." The waltz he had requested was struck up. "Do excuse me, but my blood beckons . . ."

Southby and Charles watched him move in, bow to Lady Satin and lead her out on the dance floor. "Damn, if he ain't decided on the Waverly chit!" surmised Southby with some surprise. "Steer him off, Charles, it won't do. . . ."

Charles bristled in defense of his relation. "You are out there. When did Nick ever chase after a marriageable miss? No, he is just amusing himself."

Lady Satin though did not see it that way. The fact that he singled her out for *his* first dance, and that a waltz, was most significant to her. She made up her mind that he had come to the ball for one reason: to see her again. As this was all she could have hoped to achieve, she glowed with this belief and discovered that his deep blue eyes took her to a place she never knew existed.

He was, as his cousin had stated, only amusing himself. Oh yes, she had intrigued him the day before, and yes, he found her refreshingly attractive and rather entertaining. His heart, though, was well guarded, and he was a man in total control of his emotions. She did not have the experience to tear down his defenses, and he didn't mean to take this beyond a light flirtation.

She attempted to look past his shoulder and pretend his hand wasn't holding her waist so very tightly. This proved difficult as his broad shoulders were so much higher than her eye level. Her dark eyes instead found his face and his charming smile.

He was saying in a low, oddly thrilling voice, "You look enchanting, my lady."

"Thank you, your grace, you look rather well yourself," was her open response.

He chuckled. "I see your friend the count has suffered no ill effects from his experience yesterday."

She threw her head back and giggled. "Otto? Oh, no. He is forever doing something of the sort. They call him *Deathwish* on the hunting field. The best of sports . . ."

"And lucky," the duke said on a quiet note.

"Well, that depends on how you view it all. One could say he was unlucky to find so many unfortunate situations . . ."

He cut her off, his head bending towards her ear, his lips very nearly touching her as he moved. "No, I meant lucky to be able to call you friend and have you with him so very often."

"Ah . . ." She managed to sound cool in spite of her trembling knees. "Here it is, that deadly charm Chuck warned me about."

He laughed at her unexpected remark. "Acquit me, child. I *meant* the compliment."

She pouted adorably. "Oh, then you are not flirting with me?"

He cocked his head. Here was a naughty piece, indeed. "Indeed, it would be my pleasure to do so, if I believed you wished it."

"And what woman would not? After all, you are a handsome duke with a worthy reputation," she teased. "But then, what did you call me, child? So you don't think of me as a woman?"

He eyed her. "Not think of you as a woman? You are out there. You *are,* you most certainly are, and the most dangerous kind, for you creep up on a man just when he thinks he is safe in your hoyden company."

She laughed. "Touché! Yes, I am rough and tumble, I admit it. Papa is forever wagging his tongue about my hoyden manners, but there is nothing for it. I discovered long ago that boys are able to do so many more famous things, sooo . . ."

"So you very naturally adopted their manners?" he quizzed banteringly.

She blushed and realized with some disappointment that the waltz was at an end. She also noticed that his hand remained fixed at her small waist as he led her off the floor. Sir Charles was closing in on them, and she quickly turned to give the duke her gloved hand.

"Thank you, your grace . . ."

He smiled wide and bent low over her fingers. "The pleasure, my lady Satin, was, I assure you, all mine."

"Oh, I don't know," she answered roguishly, turning away to greet his cousin Charles, who claimed her hand for the country dance.

The Duke of Morland watched her departing form. What a minx, indeed. She appeared to understand the rules and might do as a flirt this season. At least she understood that he meant nothing serious by her.

"Nick?" It was a woman's seductive voice at his back and one that he recalled all too well. He turned and found Julia's dark blue eyes gleaming warmly at him. "Oh, Nick, I had heard you were in London and have been waiting, hoping to see you." She placed both her gloved hands on his chest and lifted her tall and elegant body onto her toes, whereupon she placed a lingering kiss upon his lips. "Oh, Nick."

"Julia," he said quietly, feeling all the old memories touch him. "Julia . . . *Hartly*, now, isn't it?"

"Still smarting from that, are you?" she returned, linking her arm through his. "Well, let us see if we can make it better, shall we?"

From the dance floor Satin witnessed all this and gritted her teeth. Here was competition, indeed, but Julia Hartly? The woman was a twenty-eight-year-old widow, a tall blond beauty with the experience and style to catch a man like Lord Wildfire. What could she, a child by comparison, hope for? If Julia Hartly meant to have the duke, Satin was fairly certain Julia would have him.

As Sir Charles walked her off the floor and led her into supper she attempted an idle question. "Your cousin and Mrs. Hartly appear to be old friends?"

"Hmmm," answered Chuck absently as he wielded her through the squeeze of people. "As to that, I would have called them many things—but never friends."

"Oh?" she prompted.

"Nearly became engaged, you know, but that is another story, a long one."

"I am not running off anywhere, Chuck." She smiled sweetly.

"Curious pet." He looked at her. "Why so interested?"

"Because I *am* curious. You know me."

"Yes, I am afraid I do. Leave it be. It isn't my story to tell."

"Chuck," she said to him, "you can be one of the most provoking creatures I know."

"Next to you, Satin, I am a saint," was all he would give her besides the grape he found and plopped into her mouth.

Corine Bretton groaned as the coach she was attempting to find comfort in lurched and swayed over the badly rutted road.

"Auntie Jane . . ." She put an ungloved finger to her delicate chin and eyed her plump aunt. "Are you certain that arriving in the dead of night at Lord Waverly's will not be too presumptuous? An inner voice keeps telling me that we should have put off this visit until the morning."

"Nonsense," returned Lady Jane Bretton, "he is my brother after all, and, besides, he sent for us!"

"No, he sent for you. He isn't aware that *I* am . . ."

Her aunt cut her off. "You are my niece, my late husband's blood, and therefore you are as welcome as I." Lady Jane cast a look of appraisal at her niece. The girl was a placid creature; tall, slim and with an abundance of tawny curls that framed a heart-shaped face. She could see Corine's hazel eyes through the dim light giving her look for look. "Besides, it will be good for you to meet your cousin. I can't think why I never threw you two in each other's way before."

"I have never met Lady Satin because I spent most of my years in the United States with my parents." She smiled. "As well you know, so do not try and change the subject. Why must we charge into his lordship's town house in the dead of night? Can we not stop at a posting inn for the evening and proceed bright and early in the morning?"

"Logical, but useless. If I know my niece Satin she is attending some rout or other and will be in late with her father. Gadabouts the two of them, cut from the same mould, but darling creatures, really. They just need someone to guide them, which my sister-in-law did very well until her death. Bless and God rest her soul." She sighed. "Never mind. You, my dearest Cory, are just the one to keep Satin in line."

"Keep her in line? I don't think I want to do that to anyone . . . and besides . . ."

"Besides?" Lady Jane clucked, "No, there can be no hesitating on this score. Her father did not write very clearly on just what type of scrape she is in this time, but I fear it may be serious." Confidingly, and with a smile, she added, "He can't abide my company for long, you know, which means if he has sent for me . . . well, stands to reason it is serious business."

Miss Bretton put all this information aside and reiterated that this still did not excuse their late arrival at the Waverly town house.

"Oh, pooh! I am not about to sleep between strange sheets simply because of the lateness of the hour. Depend upon it, Waverly don't expect it of me. What he does expect is almost anything from me and that is precisely what I like to give him."

Miss Bretton could see that there would be no putting her aunt off in this regard. She gave it up and took to staring out her window at the growing number of streetlights. They were entering London. Egad! How her life had changed in the past year. She had been in a finishing school in Boston when suddenly she received news that her parents had been lost in a boating accident off the coast of Virginia. Just like that . . . wiped out of her life. She had been left with a small inheritance, a tobacco plantation in Virginia, which her parents had owned. It had been their home for four years. And there was the small estate in Romney Marsh near Rye. She had returned to England and to her aunt who lived two miles south of that estate. Together they had worked on her spirits, and she had pulled through. Now, here she was, twenty-one years old and entering London's beau monde through the good offices of her aunt.

Lady Jane Bretton gave her niece a sideways glance before she too contemplated the passing scenes from her sidewall window. Cory was a dear. She had always been fond of her. She had been planting the notion in Cory's brain that Satin was in need of a solid friend. Here was a combination. If it took, the two would make an unusual pair. She smiled to herself, for this was precisely the diversion both she and Cory needed.

Chapter Five

Satin dropped her gloves onto the central hall's ornate and rather gothic round table (a relic of the past and better days) and turned to pull a face at her father.

"Papa, as much as I do adore thee and wish to please thee, we are not living in medieval times." She was teasing, hoping to coax him out of his grim mood.

"Nevertheless, daughters are still expected to honor their fathers' . . ."

She interrupted with her eyebrow high. *"Decrees?"*

"I was about to say *wishes!*"

"And it is your wish I marry a man I don't love?"

"It is my wish you *love* a decent man who can make you happy. That man is Sir Charles—if not the count."

"Papa, try and understand. I am very fond of both men; they are my very good friends, but . . ."

"But you don't love them! Famous. You lead them on!"

Her chin went up. "I do not!"

Their housekeeper opened the kitchen door and from the recesses of the nether regions came scurrying out, her plaid wool wrapper clutched tightly round her full but sturdy form. "Lord preserve us . . . I jest got word from that stable lad down Trevor Lane that Lady Jane's coach be dropping her off any

minute before she puts it up there. My lord, my lady
. . . Lady Jane . . ."

With this announcement the door knocker
sounded resonately and father and daughter stood
stock-still as they eyed one another and then their
blustering housekeeper.

Maudly opened the door wide to find Lady Jane's
postilion, who promptly and correctly stepped aside
to allow his mistress and her charge to glide past
him into the house's central and dimly lit hall.

Lady Satin sucked in air. She adored her warm-
hearted and strictly staid aunt, but they were forever at odds. She had discovered early in life that her
aunt was a study in contradictions and could not be
easily "handled." She looked at her father and noted
with some surprise that, though irritated, he did not
seem in the least bit surprised at his sister's un-
timely arrival. What was this?

Her aunt was throwing orders over her shoulder to
her driver and her man about the luggage and the
horses, and then turned to beam at the housekeeper.

"Maudly! How well you look and how nice to see
you again. Would you be a dear and show Steverns
where he may deposit my niece's things as I will be
taking the yellow room as always."

"Yes, mum, it has been in readiness for you
though we did not expect you till tomorrow," Maudly
answered and then sniffed, thus expressing her disapproval of such an entrance at such an hour.

Lady Jane laughed and turned to her brother and
his daughter. "Well, here we are!" she announced
quite happily.

"The devil," his lordship said under his breath,
but his daughter was laughing and going forward to
give her aunt an affectionate squeeze.

"Auntie Jane, so you are, but what should bring
you at such an hour is a mystery to me." She looked
inquiringly past her aunt to the tall and obviously
embarrassed girl with her.

"What should bring us?" returned her aunt rue-fully. "Why, *you* my dear, you." With that, she went past Satin, saying over her shoulder, "Meet your cousin, my late husband's niece, Corine Bretton." Then to her brother, "Darling"—she looked him over—"you look dreadful, no doubt all your gadding about . . ."

Her voice seemed to fade into the background as Satin closed her open mouth and met Corine in silence. Both girls looked at one another and then at their aunt before something, perhaps a tickle of the situation, brought a mutually felt giggle to their lips.

"Hallo," said Satin, "how can it be that I have never met you, and no, don't try and tell me now. Let me take you upstairs, for you must be exhausted from your trip and you can tell me after you are settled in."

"That would be very nice," said Corine. She did not have time to say more, for Satin pulled at the girl's spencer sleeve and led her up the dimly lit carpeted stairs to the next landing and chattered all the while about the antics of their zany aunt.

This immediately calmed Miss Bretton, for oddly enough it made her feel at home and at ease with the sophisticatedly dressed smaller girl. She watched as Satin threw open the door to a pretty but small room done in shades of blue and soft yellow. She listened as Satin told her where things could be stored and she smiled as Satin plopped, without a care to her clothes, onto the four-poster bed.

"Now," said Satin, smiling brightly and patting a spot beside herself on the blue velvet coverlet of the bed, "take off that spencer and bonnet and be comfortable so we can talk."

"Thank you," Corine responded politely. She was by nature always cautious in her dealings with others. Here was a sprite of a woman, dressed in a most daring flame-colored gown and looking very naughty indeed, yet there was a warmth in Satin's dark eyes that touched Miss Bretton's interest.

Satin eyed the girl before her, watching her as she removed her outer garments, and heard her sigh without seeming to notice that she was doing so, and Satin chuckled. "You sound tired."

Miss Bretton pulled a face and said matter-of-factly, "I am. Wouldn't you be after spending a great many hours with Aunt Jane in a closed coach?"

"Ye Gods, yes!" exclaimed Satin feelingly.

Cory plopped onto the bed. "I am sorry for this late entrance of ours; there was just no dissuading Aunt Jane. . . ."

"Hmmm. You don't have to tell me that. I know what Aunt Jane is once her mind is made up. So tell me, why is she here?"

Cory clammed up. "Hadn't you better apply to your aunt for that answer?"

"Oh ho! You don't trust me? Come then, we are no doubt just about the same age, aren't we? I am twenty-one—and you?"

"The same, but what has that to do with anything?"

"Well, that puts us on the same side at once, doesn't it?" Satin laughed, but she could see her new cousin was reluctant to speak on the subject, so she changed it. "Never mind then. Tell me instead why we have never met before and how it is you have never been to London for the *season*?"

"I lived with my parents in Virginia," was the quiet reply. "Until last year, though, most of my time was spent in Boston at school. I was in Boston when my parents were killed in a boating accident." Her hazel eyes clouded over and she looked down at her hands now folded in her lap. "Aunt Jane has been very good to me. . . ."

Satin's soft heart immediately reached out as did her hand, and she touched Corine's shoulder. "I am sorry. Please don't talk about it if you don't want to. I understand . . . I do."

Cory gave her a wry smile. "It's over and I am fine . . . really."

Satin appraised her. "So you are, and we are going to make up for lost time and have society at your heels!"

"Oh, really?" Corine was dubious. "And how do you propose to manage that?"

"Well . . ." Satin screwed up her mouth as she thought. "There has to be an angle, you know. Beauty is never enough with the beau monde. One must ravish them, stimulate their senses . . ." She eyed her new cousin. "You are certainly pretty enough with that tawny mass of curls and your darkish skin. You are tall enough, well formed and, of course"—Satin smiled, pleased with herself—"you are an heiress!"

"I am not!" Cory objected at once.

"Aren't you?" Satin was brought down a peg. "Well, never mind, you have inherited something, haven't you?"

"Well, as to that, there is the estate in Romney Marsh and a small competence, but my dowry is not stupendous, Satin."

"But there is one!" Satin beamed. "Never mind, that is all you need."

"Why should I have to resort to such tactics?" Cory frowned. "I don't understand. Aunt Jane means to give me entrée into society. Isn't that enough?"

"Ha! You don't understand. I am not an heiress, and it is at times most depressing to find a charming fellow, a fine specimen of flesh and blood, flirt outrageously with one, only to discover that one," she pointed to herself, "has not the means to bolster his ravaged estates."

"Well, I would imagine that you wouldn't want such a terrible fellow," responded Cory, pulling a shocked face.

"Innocent! Aristocrats are a troubled lot." Satin laughed out loud. "They cannot work for a living, you see, so what must they do but marry for it!" She tilted her head mischievously. "I, for example, am expected to marry for money."

"But, how can you . . . ?"

"Aha! I am Lady Satin of Waverly, you see. So I am expected to marry beneath my class . . . sell my name and marvelous blood . . ." She waved this off. "Never mind, we are getting away from the point. The point is that you must be brought to the haut ton's attention. A little rumor of no great proportion should do it nicely, don't you think?"

"No, no, I do not think so."

"No? Well, you will."

The meeting of these two girls was very much like putting the lyric to the tune. It was inevitable that they should become fast friends for they shared a kindred spirit, a sense of humor, an appreciation of the ridiculous. They found that they were able to view life from the same height, to turn to one another and laugh, or to cry, always understanding the other's mind.

Satin did the outrageous, the bubbling, the naughty and the impulsive deeds, while Cory would observe from her seemingly placid exterior and thoroughly enjoy all. She wielded a fine hand of control over Satin, and Satin pushed Cory out of herself and drew on her sense of fun. They were a perfect pair.

Satin also started the rumor. Very easily, as well, for all she had to do was lightly mention to Otto that her cousin had come into 'something of an inheritance.' That was all that was needed. Before long it was whispered throughout the beau monde that Miss Corine Bretton was not only one of the season's lovelies, she was also wealthy. So it was that Cory's dance card was forever filled, and the two cousins fluttered throughout society most enjoyably.

Satin did not see very much of the duke, though on two occasions they did meet briefly in the park, where she was able to introduce him to her cousin. After one of these meetings she turned to Cory with a sigh and said, "I want him, you see."

"Satin!" responded Miss Bretton on a high note.

"Oh, I know what that sounds like, but I can't help it, Cory, I do." She watched his retreating form. "It is, of course, quite impossible. I am no doubt nothing but a child to someone like him. After all, he could have anyone he wants."

"Stands to reason," agreed her cousin thoughtfully. "Yet he is not adverse to your charms"—she was now twinkling— "and you did exhibit them as best as you could, didn't you?"

"Devil!" returned Satin playfully. "How could I do that with all the world watching us in Hyde Park?" She looked around her. It was the fashionable hour and, indeed, it seemed that all of London's haut ton was out displaying themselves. She sighed and would have started off had she not noticed that Lord Wildfire had pulled up his black gelding to speak to another man on a gray.

"Look!" Satin drew attention to the vision this presented.

"Look at what?" inquired her cousin reasonably. There was, at this moment, a juggler working a set of ripe apples. There, too, was a rather strange-looking gentleman balancing himself on the ledge of the water fountain whilst his friends cheered him on.

"That man with Wildfire . . . there on the dapple gray . . . see?" returned Satin on a note of excitement.

"Hmmm," responded Cory, "nice horse."

"No, you dolt. Look at the man," Satin snapped exasperatedly.

Cory saw that there was indeed a gentleman of fair countenance dressed in the required riding attire for town and responded, "So?" For she could see nothing outstanding about the man, neither the style of his clothing nor the cut of his style!

"Do you know who that is?" Satin was obviously excited.

"Satin, how could I?"

"Right you are. You couldn't, for he has been rusticating in the country for . . . oh, perhaps two years. I have never really met him, though I did see him often enough before—before it all happened."

"Before all what happened?" In spite of herself, Cory was becoming interested.

"The big scandal," said Satin portentously. "Oh, they are leaving. Fancy Wildfire and him—friends?"

"Him? Who is he?"

"Sir Frederick." Satin eyed her cousin. "You never heard the name mentioned by Auntie Jane?"

"No . . . no, I don't think so," replied Cory doubtfully.

"Well, it was all gossip, but . . . oh, I don't know if I should repeat it. After all, it wouldn't be fair to him—and I rather think he suffered enough over the ordeal. Oh, look, here comes Byron!"

Approaching them was a gentleman of average height, considerable good looks and with a decided limp to his gait. He was well dressed but had a look of general ennui about him, as though there was nothing left in the world to please him. Satin started to wave to him, but her cousin stopped her.

"Satin, don't. Your papa would be furious. Talk about a scandal . . . Byron is stirring up an entire book of scandal. Why they say . . ."

"Hush," said Satin with a laugh. "He is totally misunderstood and his only fault was that he had an affection for Lady Caro, who was naught but a doxy!" She then waved to the poet who smiled and walked their way.

Miss Bretton resigned herself and appraised the noble poet as he approached. There were certainly rumors about him, about his love affair with Lady

Caroline Lamb who was married to poor William, but it was also whispered that Byron and his half sister, Augusta, were far too involved in one another's life. However, gossip and rumor was put aside as Byron walked with them, for he was an amusing companion.

Thus, the two lively girls moved into summer aware that they were making something of a stir among the beau monde and pleased enough with the results of their efforts.

Little did they realize that things were growing from the seeds they had planted, growing to heights they had no wish to attain. Satin's mild words in Otto's ear certainly were carried on and on until suddenly it was whispered that "the Miss Bretton" was an heiress of some standing, and Satin's book took society by a storm she had never envisioned would happen!

All this while, Lady Jane Bretton moved amongst her peers and averted trouble by dropping a hint about the author's identity here and there. She would say that she had it on excellent authority that the author was a cit living on the edge of society and quite a few believed her. And then she heard that her niece, Corine, was reputed to be an heiress and with a scoff and a huff she pooh-poohed the notion, which only served to convince everyone that Corine was indeed a great heiress!

Sir Edward Danton watched all these goings-on and maintained his own council. He applied himself to the task of courting Lady Satin in high style and for all the world to observe. It was whispered that Sir Edward would indeed oust the Count Stauffenberg and win Lady Satin's hand, for the lady seemed to lean towards Sir Edward's subtle suit.

During these weeks he could not put aside the notion that Satin was indeed the author of *Passion's Seed*. There was something in the expression of her eyes whenever the book was mentioned, favorably or disfavorably criticized. There was something in the way she would avoid speaking about it, about the mystery attached to the author's true identity. There was what he already had observed about Satin's writing ability and style. Well, if she had written this novel he would just put a stop to any further advances in that field after they were married. Satin. Ah, Satin. She flitted round his mind, instigating his feelings, but would she take his suit? Would she accept him and be his wife? He had no reason to suppose otherwise. Right then, perhaps now was the moment to ask her to marry him? Yes, tonight, he thought, at the Rutledge ball.

Chapter Six

The Rutledge ballroom was full to overflowing and the hour was scarcely past ten. Everywhere jewels sparkled, candles glowed and people twirled and laughed in marked degrees. Byron came in in his languid manner, his half sister, Augusta, on his arm, and whispers went round. Then Beau Brummell strolled in and cast his comments on the wind, for he was at outs with the Prince Regent and was bold enough to remark upon it in public. Thus it promised to be a stimulating evening.

Lady Jane bustled, her brother found himself a card game and Miss Bretton allowed herself to be swept away by her numerous admirers from one country dance to another. Lady Satin, however, was not in the best of moods. To be sure, she was in fine looks with her black curls shining and framing her piquant face; her bright green gown flimsy, very nearly transparent and clinging to her provocative figure; and her cheeks as full of life as ever. Still, the corners of her cherry lips moved downwards with her thoughts. Where was he? Why did he never attend these functions? Would she ever have a chance at him? And was he in love with someone . . . the ravishing Julia Hartly, perhaps? There was a story behind that one, but Chuck had refused to tell it to her.

She managed to escape the ballroom undetected and was just turning the corner of the central hall, for she meant to step outside for a breath of fresh air, when she felt the hem of her gown being tugged and she heard the unmistakable sound of ripping material. Dismayed and surprised, she turned and, as she was doing so, heard a deep, familiar male voice.

"How clumsy of me." It was quietly said as a white-gloved hand reached out gently to take hold of her bare elbow for, indeed, it appeared as though she were slightly unsteady.

Unsteady? Faith, she was very nearly toppled over by the sight and sound of him! It was Wildfire. Here was the duke, the man of her dreams, the man she had decided to have. Here he was, ripping her gown and talking to her. What should she do? What should she say? If it had been Otto who had ripped her hem she could have, would have, laughed and called down abuses on his head. She couldn't do that to Wildfire! No, of course not. Why? Because . . . just because. So all words choked in her throat.

"It . . . is . . . really . . . nothing," she managed to stammer out.

They both regarded the fine, soft material of her gown and the enormous length of material that had been yanked away from it. She felt a fool.

He said, "It is my fault, you see, for I wanted to catch up to you before you were out of sight and stepped forward too quickly. Please allow me to help you make repairs."

He was so cool, so collected, so . . . oh, so charming. His deep blue eyes caught and held her for a long moment, and she felt herself blush. "I . . . I have some . . . pins." She shook the sequined reticule hanging from her gloved wrist for emphasis.

He lowered his voice and deftly pulled her along with him down the dimly lit hallway to yet another part of the great town house. "Pins, just what we need to set us on our way . . ." There was a teasing note in his voice and a certain light in his blue eyes.

He found a door, opened it, peered within and exclaimed pleasurably, "Ah, I don't think we will be disturbed in here!"

Where was Cory? Was this absurd? Here she was, actually alone with Wildfire, which was all she had been wanting, and she felt like a veritable schoolgirl! Cory, where are you?

She was pulled gently into a study done up in dark velvets. The room was illuminated by only two sets of wall sconces, and he remarked upon it as he placed her beside the brown-print velvet sofa.

"I hope you will be able to see," he was saying softly, taking up residence on the sofa and urging her down beside him. Then he was bending over, taking the ripped piece of material up and appraising it. "This will take some work . . ."

What did he say? He hoped she could see? See, ha! She couldn't even breathe! Her knees were shaking, so it was an excellent thing that she was sitting, but, oh, faith, his nearness was driving her mad! Nonsense. This was all nonsense. He was a man, only a man. She looked at him then, and his eyes met her glance.

He smiled. "I was hoping to see you this evening, my lady Satin." His tone was low, seductive, and he asked himself what he was doing. He had been at pains to avoid this minx. She had her family name, her maidenhood to protect her, and as he had no honorable intentions he had decided to leave her be. Right, so what in hell was he doing?

"Why?" she asked, looking at him straightforwardly and in a manner peculiar to herself.

"You know why," was all he answered as he flicked her nose.

"Do I?" She shook her head. "I haven't seen you enough to understand your meaning. Why this evening? There have been so many others in the last few weeks that you managed without . . . er . . . seeing me."

He laughed out loud. "Right you are, but I decided to give in to temptation tonight."

"Ah, so then I am temptation?" She felt herself

swing into his flirtation and she felt more at ease on this level. Here then, it was just for fun, nothing more. Safe, for the moment, she felt safe. She pulled off her gloves to remove the pins from her reticule.

He took up her fingers and put them to his lips. "You are more than that, child, you are quite dangerous as well, but I am certain you have been told that."

"Have I?" She pulled her hand out of his hold. "I don't think Otto would call me dangerous."

"Perhaps not, but I rather think Sir Edward would . . . indeed, from what I hear, you have only to move in for the kill . . ." Now why was he insulting the girl? She hadn't done anything to warrant it. Yet he found he could not help it and he wanted to know about her relationship with Danton. Rumor had it that she would take Danton's suit. Well, would she?

Something in her sizzled, and she came up from her handiwork to cast him a haughty look. "Is that what you hear, your grace? How very entertaining, to be sure." There! She had told him nothing and she was quite proud of herself, for she felt she had dealt him a surprise if he had meant to ruffle her. She looked away and applied herself to her hem.

He was amused, and his blue eyes twinkled, for he enjoyed getting a rise out of her. "That and other things . . ." he prodded baitingly.

She did not take the bait. "And do *you* listen to idle gossip, your grace? I would not have believed it of you."

He inclined his head. "I am pleased to find you have such a high opinion of me." He turned it around.

She was looking for an answer when the door opened wide and the count stuck his head in, discovered Satin on the couch with the rake, Wildfire, and nearly had a spasm.

"So," he pronounced, "here you are!"

It was precisely at that moment that Lady Jane

took her niece, Miss Bretton, to one side and asked in worried accents, "Where, dearest Cory, can that dratted cousin of yours be?"

Cory laughed. "No doubt she is just where she should be and with a perfectly good explanation."

"Humph! Well, try and tell her father that," snapped Lady Jane.

Cory smiled and said dryly, "I would, dearest aunt, if he wanted to know, but I rather think he is too steeped in his cards."

She sighed. "So he is, more's the pity. Should be looking after that hellcat of his."

"Auntie Jane! You can't call Satin a hellcat." Cory came to her cousin's defense immediately. She might in fact do so herself, but she found she could not allow others to criticize Satin.

"Oh? Can't I? Then where is she?"

"Certainly *not* raising . . . er . . . hell. If she had been, you would have heard about it by now. Trust me, I am certain there is a very good reason why she is not here."

"And that is another thing," stuck in Lady Jane, suddenly changing the subject.

"What is?" Cory had the immediate feeling that she should not have asked.

"All those fortune hunters running at your heels! It is beyond me why they should . . ." She eyed her niece suspiciously. "It is something your angel Satin has done, isn't it?"

"Aunt Jane, Farley dotes on me and he is plump enough in the pocket, isn't he? Then there is Wendell as well . . . you can't say—"

Her aunt cut her off. "I ain't a green girl. I didn't say every man waltzing you round the floor was after an inheritance you don't have. I asked why there are men like Colonel Higgens and Chesterfield forever ringing our doorbell when they are notorious fortune hunters?" Then to herself, "Not that it is their fault. They have no choice. They must align themselves with wealth if they are to save their ancestral homes." Then back to the point, "However, that is neither here nor there!"

"Oh!" Cory exclaimed, stepping forward almost convulsively. "Here comes Satin—with the count."

"Dangerous. That is what he is," said the count into his friend's small ear. "Don't want you hurt by him. Mind now, he is a gentleman and I ain't saying he would . . . well . . . actually play a May game with you, Satin, but . . ."

Satin laughed. "Stop it, Otto. He is, as you say, a gentleman, and all he was doing was helping me repair my gown, which I think looks quite neat, don't you?"

"Hmmm . . . though I can still see the rip." Otto looked her over. "Oh oh, there is your aunt—looking the very devil!"

Satin laughed. "And, judging by Cory's expression, we haven't come a moment too soon."

Sir Edward Danton was looking his very best. Even the Beau himself would have raised an approving eyebrow. Sir Edward's black velvet fit his slender form to perfection; his cravat was tied with precision; his chestnut curls gleamed round the angular face they framed. He moved with ease as he entered the ballroom, sought out the woman he was already beginning to think of as his and made his way towards her.

He was anxious and anticipating the moment when he would have her alone and take her into his arms. It wouldn't be the first time. Indeed, only the other day she had allowed him the thrill of her hand in his, the fever of a quick and most sensual kiss. Ah, Satin. She triggered his passion and he meant to have her. Business had kept him at home with his man later than he had intended, so he had found himself in a rush to get here and now, *now,* all he could think of was Satin . . . Satin.

A waltz struck up, and Otto saved Satin from her aunt's rebukes by leading her out onto the floor. Happily, Cory also found herself in a gentleman's arms; thus Lady Jane was left to stew in her own juices until later. Sir Edward frowned. Drat the count, but then perhaps he should be thankful to him for keeping Satin safe from all others. He made his way towards her, deftly getting through the squeeze and gently patting the count aside. Otto had no choice but to relinquish his prize, and Satin found her dark eyes looking up and into Sir Edward's hazel green ones.

"And now I am whole," he said softly, his eyes caressing her lips.

He was certainly attractive, and it was more than flattering to have such a sophisticated man pay her homage, flirt with her and, yes, even arouse her. She had allowed him to take her hand, to lightly kiss her lips, experimenting with her feelings, with her desires, and she found that it was not at all difficult to want him.

"And"—she flirted with her dark eyes—"satisfied?" In spite of her two seasons, at times she just wasn't aware that she was playing with fire. This was one of those times.

"No, not quite satisfied, but I will be," he answered, and his gloved hand squeezed her waist.

This was a bit too much for her sense of propriety. He was taking too many liberties, too often, too soon and besides, at the moment, there was another man in her mind's eye. She stiffened.

He misunderstood and laughed. "My dearest Satin, my adorable one, can it be that you don't know what I mean?"

She frowned. "Just what do you mean, sir?"

"I mean to have you as my wife, my lady, my . . . love," he answered on a serious note.

She nearly stumbled and looked sharply at his face. He was most definitely in earnest. She lowered her eyes, sorry for it, for now the game would have to end, and she had been enjoying it. "I am honored, Sir Edward . . . and dreadfully regret . . . that it is not possible."

He was astonished beyond belief. He had never imagined he would be rejected. Why, more mamas than he could count had flaunted their daughters at him, daughters with money! Here was this . . . child, this minx, this she-devil, openly flirting with him, leading him on to—to what, dash him to the ground? No. Perhaps she was being coy?

In the middle of the waltz he took her hand and pulled her off the floor. There was nothing she could do without creating a scene. She tried to stop him by gently pulling her hand away, but he would not release her.

"Sir"—she attempted to call him to order—"what do you think you are doing?"

"It is too hot in here. We are going for some air."

"No," she answered, "I don't think so." She tried to stand her ground.

He turned and glared darkly into her eyes. "Lady Satin, you will quietly accompany me into the garden, for I mean to talk to you *now*!"

Perhaps she owed him this. She allowed him to lead her through the open glass doors onto the stone-paved and winding path that went through the Rutledges' ornamental garden. There were torches lit everywhere, but there also were high and eye-shielding yews; he took her behind one of these ever-greens and rounded on her.

"My lady Satin, I mean you to carry my name, do you say me nay?" He was goaded into white fury.

"I would make you miserable, sir," she attempted.

He took her shoulders. "What new kick is this?"

"Please, Sir Edward, I have enjoyed your company . . . your escort these last few months, but I am persuaded we would not suit as man and wife. In time you would find my antics tiresome."

"Is that what is worrying you?" He laughed, thinking he had found the source of their problem. She wanted reassurance of his undying devotion. Women were such creatures. "Nonsense. I adore you, Satin. Haven't I convinced you of that yet?"

"Stop . . . oh, do stop . . ." She didn't know what to do now. "I—I am not in love with you, Sir Edward. I can't marry you . . ."

He went white with rage, and this time there was no tenderness in his hold. He shook the shoulders he held. "Damnation, woman! Then you will learn to love me!" He was not the sort that took rejection well.

"Let me go!" she cried, for now she was frightened. "You are hurting me . . ."

"I suggest," came a strong male voice, "you release the lady at once!"

Both Sir Edward and Lady Satin discovered the duke standing in quiet authority. Sir Edward's hands dropped to his side, but they were clenched in fists. Instinctively and without realizing she was doing it, Satin ran to Wildfire's side and clutched at his arm, one hand covering her mouth. He looked down at her, smiled and bent his arm.

"My lady, allow me to escort you to your aunt, who searches for you everywhere."

"Nick!" It was Sir Edward. "This is none of your affair and you would be advised to stay out of my way. . . ."

"Ah, Ned, you know me better than that," was all the response he was able to give at the moment, for already the minx at his side was yanking at his elbow and pulling him along and away from the scene, taking his timely rescue as her due!

They left Sir Edward fuming at their backs, and the duke stopped Lady Satin before they entered the ballroom. "Will you tell me, little terror, what you were doing with Sir Edward out here?"

She put up her chin. " 'Tis none of your"—she bit her lip—"or must I, because you were so kind . . . ?"

He laughed. "No, I won't force it from you."

She smiled. "I am a terrible girl and I am ashamed to admit that . . . I think I led him on . . . and now he is displeased with me." She sighed. "Can we leave it at that?"

"We can leave it anywhere you like, but my Charles is right."

"Is he? What does Chuck have the good fortune to be right about?" she returned.

"About you. He says you are a handful and, my little lady, you are, you certainly are, but here is your aunt, and I think she means to have a go at you." So saying, he gave her a bow and backed off.

Satin sighed and put on a smile as she waited for her aunt, who came charging full speed in her direction. Ye gods, she thought, *what a night!*

Chapter Seven

The lobby of the House of Commons was in an up-roar. There were corn laws to be fought over and the deplorable state of the economy to discuss, and there wasn't a man present that didn't have an opinion to express.

The Duke of Morland sighed as he looked around. He was waiting for his cousin, Sir Charles, and Mr. Wethering to arrive as Wethering was due to speak this morning. Eventually, he and Sir Charles would have to make their way over to the House of Lords and take up their seats, but first he wanted to speak to his friend about his intended speech. Well, and where was he anyway? Wildfire looked around, for his patience was ever short. The buzz of voices was getting louder and harder to put up with. What was all this? Talk. Nothing but talk. Always talk. So very little action, meaningful action, and he had ever been a man of action! Selling out of the Duke of Wellington's army was something he had imagined he might regret forever and it was certainly so at this moment. Ah well, he had had no choice at the time. His older brother's death some years ago had put him in line, and so when his father had died, it had precluded any other decision. Someone had to carry on the smooth running of their vast estates and that someone had always been a duke of Morland!

While the duke mused on such thoughts, a man hurriedly made his way towards the House of Commons. His name was Bellingham and he was about to make history. For some months he had been suffering from a personal grievance, and it had finally boiled over. In his inner coat he carried his pistol and in his heart an overwhelming degree of hate. He had been sent to prison in Russia. Following the course an Englishman could take, he had appealed to the British representative stationed there at the time, Granville Leveson Gower, and Gower had done absolutely nothing to aid him in his plight. During his incarceration he had gone bankrupt so that he returned to England a broken man in ill health. His grievance grew against England and Gower until he could hold it back no more.

He made his way unobserved through the street door. The duke noticed him at once for there seemed to be an air of frenzy about the newcomer and Wildfire's brow went up with interest. Bellingham stopped a passerby and the duke heard him ask for Gower.

"Not here . . . was called away on business," the passing gentleman answered politely before moving off.

"Not here? No . . . he must be . . . he was due to speak . . ." Bellingham became so distraught that the duke's interest was now keenly pricked.

"Well . . ." Bellingham's eyes took on a strange light as he found the prime minister walking towards him. "Well . . . here is England . . . here is our prime minister . . ." He withdrew his pistol, bringing it into line.

Sir Charles touched the duke's shoulder but found his hand brushed off as Wildfire realized what was about to occur. He saw Bellingham level his gun at the prime minister of England and with a startled exclamation ran forward.

"Hold!" he shouted as he charged Bellingham in a useless effort to deter him, but it was already too late. The noisy room was brought to total quiet by the reverberating boom of Bellingham's exploding pistol. The prime minister, the Right Honorable Spencer Perceval, lay still and bleeding on the marbled floor.

The Duke of Morland was aptly named, for like wildfire he seemed to be everywhere at once, doing everything. He had the gun in hand, he had Bellingham. He managed to instruct two sturdy gentlemen to take over in that regard as he bent to overlook the prime minister's wound. He was calling for a doctor, for the beadles. He was taking command and bringing the hubbub into order around him.

"Charles!" He called his cousin to his side, for no sooner had he gotten the room under some control then what must happen? Of course, it was an emergency situation, and what else would happen in an emergency situation but total chaos! Men were shouting to one another, questioning, accusing, demanding. Their prime minister had been shot, and Tories eyed Whigs with open suspicion.

Charles was there in an instant. "Here, let us take this man . . ." He was guiding Bellingham. Sir Charles now had a strong grip on him and was taking him towards the beadles, who were fast approaching.

"What is your name?" It was Sir Charles that asked.

"I am . . . I am . . ." Bellingham couldn't quite remember. "Yes, I know . . . I am Bellingham . . ." His voice was touched with a certain detachment.

"So it is," answered the duke. "Now do you know what you have done?"

"Done? Not enough. I am a ruined man." Bellingham zeroed in on his grievance. "Ruined, but I was innocent. I was sent to prison, and Gower did nought to help me. It was Gower . . . Gower I wanted to kill." He bent his uncovered head into his hands and then looked up at the duke intently. "England threw me to the dogs—it was England, too, that betrayed me."

"But why the prime minister if it was Gower you wanted?" This was from Charles.

"Why? Because Gower, sneaking dog that he is, eluded me." He pointed at the limp form of the prime minister. "Didn't dislike Perceval you know, it wasn't him . . . But Gower wasn't available you see, and the prime minister had to do . . ."

The duke and Sir Charles exchanged glances. Without a doubt the man was deranged. Bellingham was taken into custody at that point, and the duke and his cousin were left staring at one another in some disbelief.

"By God, Nick, if I didn't know better I might think all this the work of the French and their spies."

"Nonsense, Chuck. You saw the man; it had nought to do with the frogs." He turned to where a doctor was attending the prime minister. "Come." It was over, and the prime minister was dead.

It was natural and quite inevitable that the prime minister's murder would dominate drawing-room conversations and it did for some days. So it was in Lady Satin's drawing room where her Aunt Jane sat in regal placidity stitching her sampler. His lordship, the Earl of Waverly, was attempting to concentrate on Count Stauffenberg's lengthy discourse on the various problems this murder was causing the nation, and Satin sat staring out of the street window on the busy scene below.

Cory looked at the back of her cousin's dark head and sighed. Three days had passed since the Rutledge ball and Satin was in a sorry state. From all Cory had learned of her cousin's nature this behavior was totally unlike her. Satin was pining. The source of her unhappiness was Wildfire himself. For

some obscure reason Satin had decided that the duke
was forming a *tendre* for her and that he would call
on her immediately after the ball. The next morning
came and went and of course the duke did not call.
Sir Edward did and attempted to regain his ground.
He did not, and when he left, Satin confessed to Cory
that she was frightened of him. The next day came
and left without a sign of the duke, and here they
were into day three and there was still no sign of
him.

Cory attempted logic, reason and sanity in her
talks with Satin. All she could get was: "But, Cory, I
have this instinct . . . this feeling that he . . . he
could possibly love me one day . . . at least he is interested."

"Yes, so he is, but that sort of man doesn't give up
his heart easily. There are too many things dividing
his attention and, oh, Satin, what *you* want, he is
just not capable of giving."

The drawing-room door opened, and Maudly surprised the assembled group by dropping into a
bobbing curtsey and saying in regal terms, "His
grace, the Duke of Morland, Sir Charles Liverpool
and, oh, dear, I've forgotten t'other one's name. . . ."

The duke arrived with his cousin and friend at the
double doors, grinned widely, pinched the housekeeper's cheek and said with some amusement,
"Good for you, my dear. If you are to forget anyone's
name it might as well be Freddy's here."

"That's right," said Maudly, dropping a curtsey
again, "Sir Frederick Douglas."

Satin had jumped to her feet at the announcement
of the first name. She looked a picture—all wide-
eyed, her short, dark curls in a mass and framing her
piquant face. Her gown of white hugged her figure as
was the style of the day, falling in a straight line
from a high empire waist. She watched her father
welcome their callers, watched the three gentlemen
pay their respects first to Lady Jane and then to

Cory before she was able to meet Wildfire's blue eyes.

He bent his head to her proffered and uncovered hand. His lips lingered a bit longer than they should have on her knuckles. His head came back up, but he did not release her hand. "You are even more enchanting in the full light of the day, my lady."

She released a short laugh. "And you are, as ever, all too charming to believe."

He smiled for he could see the skepticism in her eyes. No fool, this little maid, yet there was something in her manner that invited him to proceed along these lines. "But, my beauty, how can you doubt the truth . . . even from my lips?"

She clapped her hands. "Very good, but"—her finger very naughtily touched his nose—"coming from *you,* a lady could never be sure just what the truth was."

This time he laughed, caught her finger and put it outrageously to his lips. Why not, he asked himself, no one was watching. Sir Charles was already involved with the count, Lady Jane and Lord Waverly. Frederick was attempting to flirt with the cousin, Miss Bretton, and this allowed him some space for his maneuvers.

"Now just who is it that has been spreading false rumors about me?" He had her hand firmly clasped in his own now.

She lowered her dark lashes (a fetching sight!) and then up they went, allowing him the full view of eyes alight with impish gleams.

"*You.* Only you." Very pointedly did she draw attention to the fact that he had her hand as she withdrew it from his hold.

"There is only one thing to be done," he answered with a mock sigh.

"Oh?" Her dark brow was up.

"Reform me, my angel." His hand went playfully

to his heart. "Make of me what you will, for I am your slave."

She laughed out loud. "Oh, do stop! I am persuaded that there isn't a female alive who could *reform* you—or enslave you."

He was suddenly serious as he looked down at her. "Right you are, my lady Satin, and how wise of you to see it."

"And do you miss the wilds of America?" Sir Frederick asked Miss Bretton as he had just learned from Lady Jane that Cory had spent some years there.

Cory eyed the tall newcomer. There was a certain attractiveness about his boyish smile. There was a quiet gentleness of manner that was interesting, but he seemed faraway, distant, and his vague blue eyes held a certain sadness. She smiled, just a bit bored with his polite conversation. "Sometimes when I think of the hunting . . ."

His eyes sharpened. "Hunting? Fox hunting? In America?"

She laughed. "Why, yes. My father kept a kennel on our plantation and we enjoyed a fairly lengthy season."

"In Virginia? Red Fox?" Clearly, Sir Frederick was amazed.

"Indeed, marvelous red foxes and grays as well. Crafty and full of sport." She eyed him. "I take it you are an avid fox hunter?"

Otto overheard. "Fox hunting? What's this? What are you arranging, Cory?" He had very quickly adopted Miss Bretton along with his Satin.

Lady Satin was drawn to this conversation and giggled. "How you can switch in midstream from the prime minister's murder to fox hunting is beyond reason, Otto."

"What is murder—even the prime minister's—

when compared to the only worthwhile sport ever discovered by man!" was Otto's response.

"I feel I should say amen," answered Sir Charles with a laugh.

That was all that was needed. It was a room full of fox hunters all ready to embark upon the sport's merits, its spoofs, its disadvantages and its glories. So the conversation went until Otto, who knew only vaguely that Satin enjoyed scribbling of sorts, said, "That would make a good story, Satin. You should write it."

She blushed when she felt the duke's blue eyes appraise her and she returned quickly, "Oh, Otto. Why me?" She realized too late that these were not the words to silence him.

"Well, because you are a writer! That piece you did a few years ago for the *Chronicle* was very entertaining. I'd wager a monkey you would have the readers splitting their sides if you recounted one of our hunting adventures on paper."

"How very cozy you all look," said Sir Edward Danton from the open doorway. "I do hope I am not interrupting a private party."

"Of course you are not," returned Lady Jane with a snort. "Come in, Edward, and stop quizzing us with that glass of yours! Where is Maudly; why did she not announce you?"

"There was a crisis of sorts in the nether regions of the house. I told the poor woman I would show myself in as I know the way so well." He dropped a perfunctory kiss upon Lady Jane's hand, nodded to the assembled company, giving Lord Waverly respectful greeting before he acknowledged Lady Satin with a flourishing bow.

"My lady . . ." He had her hand, and then her fingertips, and pressed his lips to them, his hazel eyes burning into her.

She had to admit that he was attractive in all his blue finery and that there was certainly something exciting about the style of his address. He was being audacious, and she was drawn and repulsed all at once.

Odd, she told herself, how very odd he makes you feel. "Sir Edward," she answered him softly, "how nice of you to call on us."

He was pleased by her response. He meant to make her pay for her humiliating treatment of him at the Rutledge ball, but that could come later, after she was his. For now, he still had to court her, conquer her, and there was a thrill in that thought.

"Seeing you," he whispered, "is the only thing that is worthwhile in my day."

"You are as always very gallant," she answered, again lowering her lashes. What could she do? How did one handle Sir Edward and his heat? Was he still hoping to win her hand? Or was he just attempting to regain ground and the friendly flirtation they had enjoyed in past months?

The duke was within hearing. Sir Edward's words irritated him, but Satin's response infuriated him. What was wrong with the chit? Just the other night she had refused to marry the man, and here she was still leading him on! He looked to his cousin.

"Chuck, if we are to make our appointment with the Prince Regent, we had better leave these wonderful people and trudge over to Carlton House."

Sir Edward's head turned. "No doubt Prinny is still in a tither over poor Spencer's murder."

"Well," Otto shot out, "I don't blame him in this instance. Everything must be in a muddle . . . Whigs and Tories at each other's throats . . . the Hartfords moving in . . ."

Chuck adored the count and clapped him on the shoulder. "As you say ol' boy. Everything is in mass confusion, and there is the third coalition to think about." He turned to Lord Waverly. "Do you come with us then, my lord?"

Satin's heart sank. So that was why the duke had come this morning! It wasn't to see her at all. There was a meeting at Carlton House and the Prince Regent wanted her father there as well. It was a most lowering thought. She frowned and averted her gaze as she heard Sir Frederick, Sir Charles and Wildfire take their leave. Then suddenly the duke was towering above her, making her a bow.

"Until tonight then," he said softly.

"Tonight?" She was surprised. They hadn't made plans to see one another.

"Hmmm. Tonight, at the masquerade in Vauxhall Gardens," he answered.

"Are you going to be there?" She couldn't keep the delight out of her voice. "I never dreamed you would go to such a thing."

"You are right. Ordinarily, I wouldn't. I have long since shed such needs." He gave her a long, meaningful look and then he was moving away, wondering what in thunder he was doing flirting with such a pixieish woman!

Satin watched him leave, noted that Sir Frederick made a special but futile attempt at her cousin before he came to bend over her hand. "It was a pleasure, Lady Satin. I look forward to seeing you and your cousin again soon."

"Oh? Are you joining his grace tonight as well?" Lady Satin was playing her games.

"Tonight?" Sir Frederick inquired.

"Yes, you know, for the domino affair at Vauxhall Gardens."

"Oh, I see . . . why . . . yes, I think so . . ." Sir Frederick made a spot decision. He glanced at Miss Bretton thoughtfully, but the chit seemed totally unaware of him. Odd that, he was used to more attention from the ladies. Damn if he wouldn't go! Look at her, flirting with Sir Charles. "Yes, Lady Satin. I look forward to seeing you there."

Satin saw his glance take in Cory and she smiled

to herself. "So you will. But how will you know us?"

"Oh, I don't think any man in his right mind could mistake you and Miss Bretton."

She laughed and saw him off. "Very prettily said, sir."

Lady Jane stood up, and it became apparent that she would no longer tolerate the count's and Sir Edward's company. With his lordship's departure, she dismissed the count as though he were no more than a child, but to Sir Edward she turned and gave him her hand. "So good of you to call, Sir Edward."

He bent over her hand. "So good of you to have me." He was wary of Lady Jane, and why she did not approve of him was more than he could fathom. She should be thrilled to have someone of his social standing and financial means desirous of marrying Lady Satin!

Lady Jane waited a good moment before she turned to her girls. "Well?"

They regarded their aunt doubtfully. "Well, Aunt Jane? Well what?" asked Satin.

"Do you mean to have Sir Edward, Satin, and don't play off your games. I want an honest answer for, I tell you to your head, he means to have you!"

Satin frowned. "In truth, no, I don't want to marry him, but I do . . . like him."

"Well then, you have made yourself a pot of trouble," pronounced her aunt, wagging a finger for emphasis. "The man apparently feels you have led him on and he won't take a no for an answer. I know him, Satin, and I am warning you, you had better turn him up cold if you want to get out of this muddle."

"Turn him up cold?" Satin exclaimed. "But . . . You think I am leading him on? Do *you* think that?"

"You have been kind in your fashion and because

your fashion is . . . Well, you have a natural tendency to . . . express yourself warmly, and he has been led to believe that you are not adverse to his suit." She shook her head. "He will not like to be beaten by another man."

"Well, there is no cause to worry then, for there isn't another man." Satin sighed.

"Oh, isn't there?" said Lady Jane. She had moved towards the drawing-room doors. "We'll see," was her parting shot.

Cory made certain her aunt was down the hall and up the stairs before she turned from the door and came back into the room. "What," she asked Satin, "was *that* all about?"

"Never mind. You know that I turned Sir Edward's proposal down and that he wasn't pleased. Well, Aunt Jane apparently isn't pleased either. Forget it; it will pass. What I want to know now is: *Do you like him?*"

"Who? Sir Edward? Faith, what a question! You know I don't," answered Cory, surprised, for they had already discussed Sir Edward to some extent and Satin was fully aware of Cory's opinions on the matter.

"No, dolt! Frederick. Do you like Sir Frederick?"

Miss Bretton cast her cousin a penetrating look. "What new setout is this, Satin?"

"I only wish to know if you think he is attractive," said Lady Satin with a certain meekness.

"Well, as to that, I suppose . . ." Miss Bretton seemed only mildly interested in the subject.

"I thought he was rather taken by you," Lady Satin offered casually.

"Oh, did you?" She shook her head. "Satin, your imagination will be your undoing one day!"

"Will it, do you think?" Satin bantered. "I don't know. No one in polite society seems able to connect me with that marvelous new gothic romance . . . What was it called?" She ducked the satin pillow

that came hurtling at her head and laughed with un-
bridled glee. However, she refrained from telling
her cousin that they might meet the Sir Frederick
in question that very evening. As to the duke, she
could only pray that she would really find him
there.

Chapter Eight

Vauxhall was a fairyland place alight with torches, crystals and the latest in gas lamps. Everywhere flowers were in perfect design with the landscaping. Fountains bubbled, lovers strolled, music flowed and London's high and low in society found their respective haunts and places of revelry!

On this particular evening the aristocracy had donned their masks and their colorful dominos with every intention of plunging themselves full force into their games. This sort of thing was not to Lady Jane's tastes; she had voiced her disapproval and refused to escort the girls that evening. She went a step further and in a moment of madness forgot her good sense and advised her brother that she absolutely would not allow him to take the girls to such a function.

As soon as the words were out she realized her error, but it was too late. His lordship pulled himself erect and said in the stiffest of terms that he thought her behind the times. He went on to tell her that he was all the chaperonage Satin and Corine needed and that if he wished to give them a little frolic at the Gardens, he was within his rights to do so!

Hence, Lady Satin and her cousin found themselves amidst the splendor and frivolous style of Vauxhall. Lord Waverly discovered his friends and with little regret over his decision he went to enjoy a moment with them. He took the precaution of telling the girls not to wander off, which, being what they were, they immediately did!

"Satin, this is very nearly a paradise . . ." Cory breathed as she looked around, then more like herself she added, "At least someone has tried dreadfully hard to make it appear so."

Satin laughed. "Oh, Cory, I love the way you are forever summing things up. I had forgotten you have never been here before." Then as something caught her eye she said, "Oh, look, in the arbor. They are playing the harps."

"Satin?" Cory was not looking to where Satin had directed her. "Satin, did you know that there are three rogues at our heels?"

"Hmmm. Indeed, I know. Ignore them." Satin seemed unconcerned.

"So I should be pleased to do, but one is very nearly at my elbow." She looked up at the large brute who was now smiling down at her.

"Evening, m'lovely," said the huge fellow and though he was a well-dressed man, there was the odor of gin about him. Then, too, he had a wild gleam in his dark eyes and his hair was more than windswept beneath his rakishly set top hat. "Eh, George . . ." He motioned to his friend now walking beside Satin. "What say we have us a look under their masks?"

Satin smiled sweetly at George and shook her head. "*Not* a good idea, George. You see, if you were tempted to put one finger on me or my cousin, I should have not the slightest regret in putting a hole through that silly smile of yours. It would not, of course, ruin my evening, but I rather think it would yours!"

"Ah . . ." said George, attempting sangfroid. "Whot ye want to bother wit gentry morts fer?" he asked his friend. "Lookee there, in the red gown . . ." He was already pulling his friend off.

The third fellow simply and without a word followed suit.

Cory turned on her cousin. "Satin, you are the most complete hand! Never say you brought your little pistol with you?"

"As a matter of fact," said Satin, just a wee bit sheepishly, "I meant to, but I forgot it."

Cory raised her hazel eyes heavenward. "Give me strength enough to keep my hands off her neck." She returned her gaze to her cousin's unperturbed countenance. "You mean you . . ."

"Bluffed them. 'Tis done all the time in poker," supplied Lady Satin glibly.

"But you executed it beautifully," said a masculine and all-too-familiar voice at Satin's back.

The power of his voice brought her spinning round. Gone was her self-assurance, her two seasons' worth of sophistication. Here was Wildfire with his glittering blue eyes and his all-mighty charm. He had donned a black domino and mask, but Satin knew him at once. She knew the height and breadth of him. She knew the style of his movements, the very aroma of him, and her heart very nearly stopped beating. Ludicrous girl, she told herself silently. How did he know her? Her hair, Cory's hair perhaps, (for they had not worn their hoods) may have given them away. She offered him her gloved hand and as he took it up she managed to give him a pert curtsey.

"Your grace," she said softly in greeting.

"And so, dark eyes, you know me?" he returned, only a little surprised and ridiculously pleased.

"Anywhere," she answered flirtatiously. "There is that something special in your mien."

He now had her hand nearly to his lips. He stopped at that and looked deep into her eyes. He couldn't have the chit taking his attentions too seriously. That would not do, yet he couldn't at this moment draw back. "I am flattered," he answered her quietly, then found that one slight tug at her glove was enough to remove the offending lace thing. He placed a lingering kiss upon her wrist and then another on the collection of fingers he held in his firm grasp. "For I, too," he then said on a lower note, "would know you anywhere."

Someone moved at his back, and he turned suddenly and smiled. "Oh, Frederick, I was forgetting you."

Sir Frederick wore a domino of black and white and a white mask, and he looked striking as he strode forward and made a sweeping bow to the ladies. Cory considered him for a long moment as he went up to her.

"How is it you two are wandering about alone?" Sir Frederick asked. "No Lady Jane standing attendance tonight?"

"My father is here," said Satin, smiling, "somewhere . . ."

The duke pulled a rueful expression. "You really shouldn't wander off that far from him at Vauxhall, as well you know . . ." He was speaking only to Satin for he had taken her hand, which was still ungloved (he had slipped the frilly glove into an inner pocket of his domino).

She was all too aware of her hand in his, of the feel of his fingers clasped around her own, and she felt for a moment that she couldn't breathe. Absurd girl, she told herself, suck in air and find something to say. "I do know, but more than that I also know that I am well able to take care of myself."

"Oh ho, independent minx, not everyone will frighten off so easily," he retorted.

She smiled and a teasing note was in her voice. "*You,* for instance?"

He looked at her thoughtfully for a moment and then said quietly, "I know the rules of the game and won't get burnt, what about you, Satin?"

She eyed him. "I have never been burnt before. I

don't intend to be now, but, your grace, I haven't decided to play." With that she released a tinkling ripple of laughter.

He smiled, but he was disturbed. The chit seemed all too taken with him. Naturally, he was pleased. He was a man with a man's ego, and it was an excellent sensation to have such a bubbling and lively beauty attracted to him. However, he was not going to be taken in by any female, especially not this wild thing with her open and easy manners. She would not be easy to control. . . .

At about the time the duke led Lady Satin down the tree-lined promenade known at Vauxhall as the South Walk, Lady Satin's father cast a watchful eye about for his daughter. She was nowhere to be found. This was because he was still very near the main entrance known as the Grand Walk and that was where he meant to stay until Satin and Cory returned to him.

He frowned and scarcely attended to his cronies' ribald remarks as the thought occurred to him that Satin might find a bit too much mischief in the wilds of Vauxhall. What would Lady Jane say if Satin and Cory raked up a bit of scandal? Would they? No. Not Cory at any rate, and certainly his Satin knew where to draw the line.

"Waverly?" Lord Carlisle bent his gray head. "Didn't you hear me? Look, isn't that the Jersey coming to us?"

Waverly groaned. "So it is, and what she could want is more than I want to find out!"

Lady Jersey approached and pinched Lord Waverly's cheek. "Tell me, Waverly, where is that imp of yours?"

"Satin? Why . . . what makes you think she is here?" returned his lordship cautiously. Lady Jersey had the power to ostracize or to admit the gently born ladies to Almack's. He didn't want his Satin to fall from grace.

She eyed him quizzically. "My dearest Waverly, knowing Satin as I do, there is not the slightest doubt in my head that she is here. She could never stay away from such a frolic. What I want to know is how you could allow her to wander off alone?"

"Didn't," he answered pugnaciously, "she ain't alone." He was not, in actuality, telling a lie, but had he known she was at that moment being managed by Lord Wildfire into the darkest corner of the South Walk, he would have felt his knees quake and his temper rise.

Three triumphal arches loomed, and Satin remarked upon the fineness of the spectacle against the black, star-lit sky.

"Hmmm, but a bit overdone," returned the duke softly. He didn't have to glance around to know that a step off to the side of the walk would bring them behind a set of high pyramid yew trees. He took the step and Satin's elbow; he said huskily, "And nothing to the fineness of your bright eyes."

It happened too quickly to stop him. Did she want to stop him? Of course. Didn't she? Without a doubt. If her arms went round his neck, it was only to catch her balance. If her lips parted to receive his kiss with sweet response, it was only because she did not want to appear gauche and childish, and, oh, but he felt so lean, so hard, and she felt so weak.

He came up from that kiss and smiled. He was so sure of himself, so much in control. "Come . . . I must return you to your father and cousin."

"My cousin?" Who the devil was he talking about? Her senses were reeling from the embrace and here he was talking practically. "Oh! Cory . . . of course . . . yes, my father . . ."

He was aware of her confusion and for some inexplicable reason he felt more than the usual satisfaction in his ability to arouse a lovely woman. She was a child; she was not someone he should be taking advantage of yet, at this moment, it was difficult not to. He flicked her nose.

"That is unless you would rather walk deeper into the wood and . . ." He didn't finish the sentence, but let it drift into a smirk.

She took instant umbrage. "You are very sure of yourself." Her dark brow was up.

"And you"—he made her a flourishing bow—"have given me reason to be."

He was insufferable. All the more so because it was true. She found herself back in control because her ire was up. "Don't mistake my dallying with anything more than that." She put on a coy smile. "I have this insatiable curiosity you see and wanted to find out myself if the rumors about Lord Wildfire were exaggerated!"

He frowned. Was this so? He looked deeply into her dark eyes and had the gratification of making her blush. Very well, he would play her game. "And . . . ?"

She turned and then over her shoulder she said, twinkling, "Oh, I don't know . . . I may need further investigation. . . ." With that remark she giggled mischievously before tripping lightly off and away from him.

He was after her in a moment, had her tightly in his grasp for her playfulness had aroused him. However, as he was about to give her more food for thought, a jolly voice with a deep German accent called out, "Satin? Satin . . . is that you?"

They turned to find Otto, his domino askew and his mask in his hand, coming towards them.

During this time, Sir Frederick was attempting to engage Miss Bretton's wholehearted attention and was having a difficult time of it. He was deft in the art of dalliance and frowned to find that she did not pick up on any of his flirtations. She seemed either totally oblivious or disinclined. This was, for him, a singular experience. He finally laughed and said, "I can see you don't mean to be won over by any of my tricks."

That got her attention. She looked into his pale blue eyes for a long moment, and one fine, light brow went up quizzically. "Have you been trying to trick me, sir?"

He laughed again and this time flicked her nose. "Certainly not! I have been trying with the utmost care to seduce you."

She smiled. "Really? I wouldn't have guessed."

He put a hand to his heart in a mock show of pain. "Wounded! Ah, gentle maid, do you know what you have done to my pride?"

She laughed. "You should be flattered, sir. I have been thinking what a gentleman you are."

"And so I am," he said hurriedly to assure her. "But even a gentleman, when assaulted by such beauty, may be overcome to do the unthinkable."

"What unthinkable thing is that?" Cory was ever practical in all things, but her eyes now twinkled as she found herself suddenly in the mood to respond to this absurd young man with the charming smile.

His answer was such that it took Cory by surprise. Easily, and with a certain gentleness, he took her chin in his fingers and tilted her face upwards first to meet his gaze. With certain deftness he dropped the softest of kisses on her well-shaped lips before standing back a touch, as though to observe the results of his handiwork.

Miss Bretton, unlike most unmarried misses he had known, did not become flustered, outraged, coy or shocked. She looked up at him consideringly and said, "I would not describe that as unthinkable. *Presumptuous,* but not unthinkable."

Sir Frederick Douglas was delighted with this chit. He burst out laughing and informed her that

she was a treasure unlike any other and that if she
didn't wish him to become even more "presumptuous" they had better find her cousin, Lady Satin.

Otto was spluttering in a fit of temper no one was
able to understand yet. Satin turned to Sir Charles,
who had trailed after the count, and opened her eyes
askance at him. Sir Charles laughed, recouped himself and made an attempt to explain.

"Lady Haversham got her bottom pinched," was
what he said.

Satin's dark eyes rounded, and even Lord Wildfire
found himself amazed. "Lady Haversham?" ejaculated Satin. "Lady Haversham's bottom?"

"Bottom," confirmed Sir Charles with a nod of his
head.

"But why would anyone want to . . . to . . . and
what does it have to do with Otto?"

"Thought I did it!" cried the count. "I wouldn't do
such a thing even if she had a bottom worth
pinching!" The notion of his being accused of such a
crime against society's oldest lioness set him spluttering again.

"Well, what happened?" Satin was looking from
the count to Sir Charles in some amusement.

"Otto happened to be just behind her. She whirled
round, ripped off his mask, scolded him for his daring
and then patted his cheek and told him that she understood how it was when a man was moved to
passion. . . ."

"Blaaah . . . uck . . ." came from Otto in a marked
degree of disgust.

"Otto proceeded to tell her that he didn't,
wouldn't, couldn't, but she would have none of it.
She thinks Otto has formed a passion for her. Has it
spread round all of Vauxhall by now!"

This sent Otto off into a convulsion that created a
havoc of indecent mirth among his friends. Miss
Bretton and Sir Frederick arrived and the story was

recounted for their pleasure, and so the night progressed.

It was hours later when Cory heard a knock at her bedroom door, but before she could give permission to enter, Satin was already within. "Cory . . . Cory. Are you awake?" Satin groped through the moonlit room and found one poster of the bed.

"I am now," Miss Bretton returned dryly.

Satin plopped herself down on the bed with a giggle. "Good. We didn't have a chance to talk."

Miss Bretton sat up and arranged her pillows comfortably. "Hmmm," she agreed, for she, too, wanted to discuss the events of the evening. "You, first."

Satin eyed a leftover biscuit on the nightstand and reached for it. "Uh-uh. I want to know all about Sir Frederick."

Miss Bretton shrugged in a manner all her own, and her expression was unreadable. "How can I tell you what I don't know?"

"Don't be provoking, Cory!" her cousin admonished severely. "Now tell me."

"Tell you what?" Cory could be a hard case.

"Very well, what were you doing alone for so long?" returned Satin sweetly.

Miss Bretton smiled. "Talking."

"Talking? Excellent, most of us do that when in company. I suppose you were walking as well? Talking and walking. Lovely." Satin smiled. "Fine. Shall I tell you what I was doing?"

"I know what you were doing," returned Miss Bretton pugnaciously. "You were attempting to conquer Wildfire's heart." She grew serious for a moment and touched her cousin's hand. "Forget him, Satin."

"But, Cory, I can't." Satin was surprised by her cousin's gravity. "Why? Don't you think he likes me?"

"Oh, he likes you and I think he wants you, but,

Satin, he won't marry you. He doesn't wish to be tied down, and he is a man used to being on his own and getting his own way. This is going to hurt you, Satin."

"I can take a little hurt," Satin answered.

Cory sighed. "I suppose . . ."

"He kissed me," Satin offered dreamily, "and then he didn't try to again. Doesn't that indicate he cares?"

"No. It indicates that he lost himself for a moment and overstepped by kissing you! Satin, you are not some backstairs wench. You are Lord Waverly's daughter, and dukes cannot go about kissing their fellow peers' daughters without paying a price."

"Oh, pooh. We are in modern times. Things are different." Satin frowned and then waved this away. "Cory . . . Oh, never mind. Tell me, do you like Sir Frederick?"

Cory eyed her cousin for a long moment. She wanted to tell her about the kiss, but she didn't want Satin's imagination to run away with her. "He is very nice . . . a bit of a flirt and in a way that comes up on you suddenly."

"How suddenly?" Satin zeroed in.

Cory laughed. "He did manage to kiss me, but"— she held up her hand to still her cousin—"it was the veriest thing . . . nothing really and only done in playfulness."

"He likes you," said Satin. "I saw it the first time he discovered you."

"Nonsense."

"Do you like him?"

"Don't be absurd, Satin. I don't even know him," returned Miss Bretton, but if she allowed herself to question her heart, she would wonder at herself. Why did the memory of that silly little kiss cause a flutter of the nerves? Why, indeed? "Go to bed, Satin. We have to get up early and get things in order before we leave for Brighton."

"I shall go, but I don't think I will get any sleep."
Satin sighed, and when she reached the door she
turned and said into the darkness, as much to herself
as to her cousin, "Don't think I mean to give up,
Cory, for I don't!"

So it was that on the next morning the Waverly
household set off for Brighton; Sir Edward set off for
Mr. Murry's offices in Soho, and the gleam of deter-
mination in his eyes boded ill for Satin!

Unaware that that particular suitor was in hot
pursuit, Satin seemed in high spirits as she rode
with her cousin some distance ahead of the coach
that held her father and aunt. Some of their servants
and most of their luggage would be conveyed by
Lady Jane's carriage later that morning. The day
was extremely fine, and a refreshing breeze whipped
at their faces as they cantered comfortably along the
main pike.

"I don't like riding sidesaddle," announced Miss
Bretton. "In the States I was young enough to avoid
censure when I rode astride."

"Well, as a rule I don't ride sidesaddle. At least,
not when we hunt. But in town and on the main road
. . . well, one must maintain the proprieties," returned Satin, then her mirth pealed out over the
statement. "At least we won't have to jump fences on
the pike for I never have mastered the knack riding
sidesaddle." Then in a tone of ultimate glee she exclaimed, "There! I told you I saw his coach!"

"Satin, don't. I'll be so embarrassed . . . Satin . . ."
objected Miss Bretton.

Lady Satin had spotted Sir Frederick's coach some
moments before and now nothing would do but to
catch up to it. "Don't be ridiculous. We certainly cannot be accused of flying to Brighton in his wake, now
can we? He knew that we were due to leave London
this morning, didn't he?"

"Well, as to that, you certainly made a point of announcing it last night, didn't you?" Miss Bretton said dryly.

"My dearest pudding heart, one must make the effort." Lady Satin laughed, not at all abashed.

Miss Bretton watched her cousin charge forth and sighed. She was not about to follow suit. In fact, she slowed her horse to a trot and patted her tawny curls into place beneath her dark silk top hat. She adjusted the well-fitted riding jacket, smoothed the silk of her skirt, fluffed the ruffle of her lacy white collar and told herself that this was all nonsense.

Satin brought in and steadied her horse as she rounded the bend and discovered the coach moving slowly along. It would be an easy thing to overtake it and shout them to a merry halt, but it was not the thing. She had screwed up her mouth as she made the attempt to think this thing out when fate came to the rescue. The coach made a horrible creaking sound, and suddenly a rear wheel was off and rolling into the woods flanking the road. In the next moment the coach was on its side and its driver hanging from the rigging.

"Faith," Satin breathed out loud and urged her horse forward. The driver was jumping to his feet and calling out to the occupant as Lady Satin drew her horse up. "Sir Frederick, are ye hurt?" the driver called sharply, for no sound came from within.

There was no response to this, and as the driver rushed to open the door of the sadly tilted carriage, Satin hopped nimbly down from her horse and allowed the animal to graze as she hurried to have a look.

The door was jammed and it was a moment before the driver got it opened. It swung upwards and away from the driver's strong thrust, and Sir Frederick's leg fell limply out. The driver and Lady Satin looked at each other and then at the crumpled body of Sir Frederick.

By this time, Miss Bretton had arrived on the

scene, and she took strong command. First she teth-ered both horses to a nearby tree before coming to have a look.

"Don't move him," she cautioned as she came for-ward. They could see that he had sustained a head wound just above and behind the ear and that a con-siderable amount of blood was oozing out down his neck and over his torn traveling coat.

"Cory, we need something to stop the bleed-ing. . . ." Satin was frowning, looking at her cousin.

"When our coach comes along, our driver can help get him out of there and we will attend to his wound then." She went thoughtful. "What we need is a place to take him."

"There is an inn down the road—and a village not far past there. I could ride for help . . . have a doctor sent to the inn." Lady Satin was already going to her horse.

"Satin, wait . . . What do you think you are doing? You can't just ride off alone. Satin . . ."

Satin was already settled in her saddle and urging her horse forward. "Cory, you see to him and meet me at the inn. Papa will not be overcome with joy, but there is nothing for it, is there?"

Cory watched her in some consternation. This was dreadful. Satin riding off alone, Sir Frederick uncon-scious and the unkempt driver looking at her as though she would make everything all right once more. However, Sir Frederick groaned and she went to him at that moment.

"Dear sir, please do not move," Miss Bretton cau-tioned him, one hand on his shoulder.

"Wha-what . . . happened?" Sir Frederick asked feebly.

"There was an accident. Your coach lost a wheel, and you sustained a nasty gash to your head. Now, if you will but lie still, my uncle's coach will be along soon and between us we shall contrive to get you safely out of your vehicle and into ours."

"Non-nonsen-se"—he attempted to sound authoritative—"I can manage . . ." with that statement he made the attempt to rise. This sent a spasm of pain through his limp arm that made him reel backwards once more. He felt himself slipping, felt the surroundings recede as a blackness enveloped him, and once more he was unconscious.

"Oh, no . . ." Cory was distressed. She looked round for her uncle's coach. "Where are they? How can they be so far behind . . . Aunt Jane, please do hurry. . . ."

Satin put away ground in a heady canter and arrived some ten minutes later at the Red Hart. The inn was a quaintly styled building brightly painted in red and white and landscaped with potted plants of various shades. Its total effect was most charming, but Satin didn't have the time to admire it as she jumped off her horse, handed the reins to the boy who came running from the inn's small coach house and rushed into the main hall of the inn.

The innkeeper, a chubby individual with a shock of gray hair and a clean white overall apron, came ambling forward for he could see the young lady was somewhat flustered. "Eh now, miss, is somethin' amiss?"

"Yes," Satin answered breathlessly. "Please forgive me, but I am pressed for time. There was an accident down the road and a friend was injured. My father will be bringing him along, and they will need someone to repair the coach, and I have to find a doctor."

The innkeeper blinked. "Whot's that ye say?"

His lady came forward as she had eyed Satin curiously from the back regions of the inn. To her Satin looked to be aristocracy, but what the girl was doing unescorted and on horseback she couldn't say, and they did not cater to courtesans at *her* inn!

"Jest hold a minute," said the innkeeper's wife, "whot's towards here?"

Satin didn't have the patience, but she realized that perhaps she hadn't been clear. "I am Lady Satin Waverly," she said in her court voice. "My father and my aunt, Lady Jane, will be here shortly with Sir Frederick, who was injured in a coach accident. If you will be kind enough to direct me to the nearest doctor, I would appreciate it."

"Lord 'ave mercy!" ejaculated the innkeeper's wife. "O'course, m'lady . . . right away, m'dear." She turned to her husband and, in snappier tones, commanded, "Don't be standing there like a lobcock! Git Tom from the cellar, he can clean it up later after he sees to her ladyship's coach—"

"No, no, it isn't my coach. It's Sir Frederick's, and I think a blacksmith will be needed actually," Satin put in. "But perhaps your Tom can be sent for him . . . ?"

This would mean a great deal of cash. There would be dinner for everyone and no doubt some coins in appreciation for their help. Yes, the innkeeper's wife was pleased enough to send Tom anywhere Satin wished. "Come then"—she turned to her husband and, with a movement of her head, sent him after Tom—"the lad will fetch the smitty, and would ye be wanting my Jack to fetch the doctor fer ye?"

"No, you have already gone to so much trouble. If you could just point me in the right direction, I think I might be able to find him, for I have traveled this road before . . ." She was attempting to recall where she had seen the doctor's fingerpost in the past.

"Haley Lane then, his cottage is jest off Haley Lane, across the way from Bleinham Grange." She frowned and eyed Satin. "The road is awful bad, though—and overgrown. Doc now, he mostly uses the back roads on his rounds, but if you take the main pike about a mile down, you'll see Haley Lane."

So it was that Satin took the main pike for more than a mile and still did not find Haley Lane. There didn't seem to be a fork in the road and the mistress of the Red Hart had been adamant that there would be a fork in the road. She went up farther and finally decided that the dirt bridle path that meandered into the woods was what the woman had meant. She took it and stopped after some yards were put away.

Squire Bleinham had been an old friend of her father's, and they had visited Bleinham Grange many years ago. Why couldn't she recall just where it lay? Perhaps a shortcut through the woods would put her near it.

She weaved her horse through the thick of the woods, jumping logs and sideswiping bushes, then she breathed a sigh of relief. There, through the clearing of the woods, lay a road dividing her present sylvan setting with a sloping grassy plain whose peak exhibited the Tudor-fashioned Bleinham Grange.

She urged her horse forward, and his trot was heady as they approached the road. It was at this moment that a high-perch phaeton of considerable style was executing the bend in the road with neat precision. Satin's gelding saw something coming at him from the corner of his eye and spooked sharply to the left just before he took the ditch between the wood and the road. Satin lost her seat, and it occurred to her that if she didn't hold on to her horse she would find herself in the ditch. With a strength that amazed her, she held to neck and mane and though she lost her dignity she managed to stay with her horse.

The driver of the high-perch phaeton cursed softly before pulling his spirited pair of grays to a halt. He handed the reins to his small tiger at the back of his vehicle with a clipped order to "hold them steady." Then he jumped nimbly down from his driving seat and went to the lady, his abuse hot and ready.

"What you need, minx, is a spanking!" said the

well-dressed, tall and rakishly good-looking Duke of Morland. "What the devil do you mean riding your horse out of the woods like a bat out of . . ." He managed to regain his composure at this stage and steadied his temper with: "You should know better. I thought you a better horsewoman than that!"

Satin was, for a moment, dumbfounded by Wildfire's (unexpected) presence. This was, however, overset by his rudeness and his insult. Her ire came to the fore, and her dark eyes blazed. She presented quite a picture with her dark green silk top hat askew, a smudge of dirt across her white cheek and her green riding jacket torn from collar to shoulder.

"I? Well! What about you? Speeding round a corner like that! And besides, what in blazes are you doing here?"

"What I am doing here is not the issue at hand," he returned irritably. "What are *you* doing here? What, in fact, are you doing charging around the woods alone when you should be on your way to Brighton with your family?"

Her chin was up as she took umbrage at his question. "What *I* do need not concern you, your grace."

"If you hadn't thrown yourself in front of my horses, it wouldn't concern me." He was already lifting her out of her saddle and was standing her before him.

She wanted to struggle against this autocratic move, but it would have proved useless, and therefore she did not resist. Nor did she object when he smoothed a stray dark curl away from her eyes and wiped the dirt from her face with his handkerchief. However, when he attempted to place her top hat correctly on her head, she swiped his hand away.

"Stop that!"

His blue eyes were glittering with amusement now. "Having told one another off in famous style, perhaps we may now discover what you are doing barreling through the woods alone," he said in an assuaging tone.

She wasn't quite ready to relent, but, oh, it was good to have him here just when she had been feeling rather worried and lost.

"You could have killed me. . . ." She thrust at him still.

"No, as I said, you are too good a horsewoman," he returned.

"Well"—she was willing to compromise now—"I suppose I really should have been more careful. I was just so happy to find the road and the grange and, oh, Nick"—she used his given name without thinking—"I have got to find the doctor and bring him to the inn."

He frowned and took her shoulder. "What's this? What's amiss?"

"Sir Frederick . . . he was hurt when his carriage lost a wheel, and they will be bringing him to the Red Hart, but I have got to find the doctor and I'm not sure where . . ."

"Come on, minx." He had her hand and was leading her to his open phaeton; then putting his hands on her waist, he hoisted her up from behind. He went and got her grazing horse and tethered him at the back of his vehicle before hopping up beside her on the seat and taking up the reins.

"Do you know where he is? The doctor, I mean?" she asked him wonderingly.

"I do," he answered and gave her a reassuring smile.

"Oh, Nick," she returned with a relieved sigh, and then as an afterthought hit her, "but what *are you* doing here?"

"Why, coming to the rescue, of course," he answered and tweaked her nose.

Chapter Nine

"Oooohoooo . . ." Sir Frederick groaned impressively and put a hand to his aching head as he drifted back to reality.

"Lie still, sir, and try not to speak just yet," ordered Miss Bretton in firm accents.

He opened his eyes and found her face, blurred but pleasantly just above his own. He wondered where he was and attempted to smile. "Hallo . . ." he managed. "What . . . what has happened?"

"Your carriage lost a wheel and as a result you have sustained some injuries," she answered him obligingly. "Ah . . ." She heard the sound of a carriage. "Here is my uncle . . ." With that she jumped deftly out of the tilted carriage and ran out onto the road waving her hand frantically for the coach to stop.

Jenkens, the driver of the Waverly carriage saw Miss Bretton at once and cooed, "Blimey now, whot 'ave we 'ere?" Then to the brother and sister within, who were in the heat of battle over fashion's latest *on-dit* and its importance, he called out, "Lookee, m'lord! 'Tis Miss Bretton and a brace of trouble . . ."

This caught Lady Jane's attention as well as Lord Waverly's, and both attempted to gain the window at the same time. Brother forgot his gentlemanly manners and shoved sister aside to exclaim, "It's Sir Frederick's coach . . . nearly overturned . . . looks as though it's lost a wheel."

"Let me see, you old whopstraw!" said Lady Jane, out of patience with him.

"Whopstraw?" His lordship pulled himself erect in his seat. "You, you stiff-rumped, bear-leading harridan!"

So it was that while brother and sister favored one another with some serious name-calling, Miss Bretton took command of the situation. She managed both Jenkens and Sir Frederick's man with gentle ease, and in a composed fashion had these excellent men carry Sir Frederick to her uncle's coach. There, Sir Frederick was eased into place. However, this caused him so much pain that once more he blacked out.

Cory was distressed and feared that he had sustained some very critical injuries. She exclaimed as much to her aunt, who broke off the battle with her brother to look over the young gentleman thoughtfully.

"Russell's lad . . . had some falling out with society some years ago . . . secluded himself for a time. Too bad his taking a spill just now. People are bound to talk."

"Aunt Jane!" Clearly, Miss Bretton was taken aback. "What can you mean? He has had a carriage accident. Why should people talk about that?"

"Ah, people do, you know. They will say he was probably driving at a breakneck speed with little regard to his name and position."

"But he wasn't even driving!"

"That doesn't matter," her aunt answered pragmatically. "People will say he was—or that he forced his man to the pace." She shrugged. "He is very pale. Come on then, let's get in and get started. He must be seen to at once." She turned to her brother. "Are you coming, Waverly?" she asked in frigid accents. "Or do you mean to stand and fume all day?"

Lady Satin looked at the duke's profile and wasn't aware of the admiration exhibited in her eyes, in her smile. He caught the look and, for some absurd reason, it tickled his ego into full swing. He sent her a quick smile and a long, "Y-es?"

She laughed. "I was only thinking how well you handle the reins."

"Thank you." He was aware that he sat taller in his seat.

She sighed. "I am ever so glad you came along." Then she cast him a doubtful look, for she wasn't sure if she should voice her next question. Something pushed her to do so. "I don't quite understand though . . . ?" It was a leading statement.

"What don't you understand?" He took the bait.

"Last night, when I mentioned that I would be leaving London for Brighton this morning, you said that you would not be setting out for Brighton till next week." She frowned. "And even if you changed your mind and were on your way to Brighton, you were going the wrong way when you nearly knocked me off the road." She peeped at him after this last statement.

"When *you* nearly landed yourself in a ditch by barreling in front of my phaeton, I was not on my way to Brighton," was his answer, and he grinned, knowing in advance that this would not satisfy her.

She waited a moment. So he did not want to tell her where he was headed. Perhaps he was in the area because of a woman. She felt suddenly depressed and turned away to contemplate the countryside.

He tilted his head in her direction and, for a reason he did not think out, decided to tell her what she wanted to know. "I was on my way to visit the old squire. He was a friend of my father's, and I had promised to give him a few days. I am promised to him for the weekend."

She brightened at once, and her dark eyes sparkled as she responded, "Oh, and then you will proceed to Brighton?"

"If that is where *you* will be . . ." His smile lit his blue eyes and his tones were caressing.

"You do that so well," she returned. "I am certain I have never heard anything to its like and yet something, I know not what, prompts me to disbelieve."

"Ah, Satin, I would that you would trust me. You can, you know."

"Lord Wildfire. That is what you are called and with good reason I am told. Yet you would have me trust you?"

"What have they told you? It's only a name my fellow officers and men gave me during our fighting in the Peninsula."

"Otto told me that you also have a reputation for going through women like wildfire," she bantered, her lips curved, her dark eyes teasing.

He laughed. "Perhaps that is so. Otto had no business telling you that. What was he doing, warning you off me?"

She smiled. "Of course. *He*, you see, *is* a friend."

He looked at her a long moment. "I suppose I wasn't very sincere in my dealings with women. That doesn't mean I am not sincere now."

She frowned. "Don't, please. You see, I believe there is a fine line between light dallying and setting out to seduce a maid. Have fun with me if you like, I am rather enjoying it, but don't cross the line." She looked full at him. "Don't go after my heart; that wouldn't be any fun."

He gave her a steady gaze. "Satin, you seem to know enough to know there are certain rules, and if we adhere to those rules, your heart won't be in it."

"You mistake. I am afraid that I am not quite that sophisticated yet." Then, to get away from a subject that was beginning to hurt . . . for what was he saying?

Was he saying that his heart was *not* in this flirtation? Of course that was what he was saying. He wanted her, but not on any permanent basis. "Are we nearly there yet?"

He looked at her hard, aware that she wanted to digress, aware that something had passed between them that had left her distant and him uncertain. "We are," he said meaningfully, hoping to win a bantering response.

She refused to pick up on it and started chattering about the accident instead. She wanted to feel at ease with him again and therefore avoided his eyes for the rest of their ride.

Sir Frederick was carried up the stairs and laid on an oversized four-poster single bed. He groaned, and Cory took up the wet compress she had prepared and applied it to his head. Her uncle was below attempting to calm his state of mind; her aunt was ordering a private parlor for their lunch.

Sir Frederick opened his eyes and found Cory above him. "You . . . are too good . . ."

"Yes, I rather think so." She smiled at him reassuringly.

He tried to sit up, and she objected. He countered, "I can, honestly, I can sit . . ."

"I am sure that you can, but just think how much more pleasurable it will be if you remain lying down."

He gave her a wry grin. "That is the best proposition I have had in some time."

"Well, thank you, sir. If you are very good and do everything you are told, I shall try and better it."

He looked full at her. "I think, Miss Bretton, that I love you."

"You only think so? By the time I am finished with you, Sir Frederick, you will be sure of it." She laughed and got to her feet to call to the chambermaid she saw passing in the hall. Satin should have been here with the doctor already. She was dreadfully worried for Sir Frederick looked too pale and there was swelling in his lower arm. She was fairly certain he had broken it.

Chapter Ten

Miss Bretton had not been wrong. Sir Frederick had sustained, in addition to minor bruises and lacerations, a broken arm. This the doctor had set by putting a piece of wood between Sir Frederick's teeth and telling him to bite hard as he snapped the bone back into place. A splint had been placed and the arm neatly wrapped. As a precaution, Sir Frederick was ordered to stay in bed for at least three days.

"I don't think we should leave him," Miss Bretton voiced quietly to her aunt. "It just wouldn't be right. What if he should suffer a fever? He has no one here to look after him . . ."

Lady Jane considered her niece thoughtfully. Sir Frederick's past was shaded by scandal and this was not a connection she wanted for her gentle Corine. However, she, too, felt that they just couldn't abandon the man. Before she could answer, Satin stuck in her considered opinion.

"Honestly, Aunt Jane, I just came from his room, and his forehead felt terribly hot to me." She looked steadily at her aunt and avoided her cousin's inquiring eye. "However, you and Papa needn't put up here."

"Well, your father needn't, that is for certain," said Lady Jane, making a spot decision. "I will send him off immediately after we have eaten our luncheon. He may see that the house is in readiness for us in Brighton. Indeed, perhaps we shall do very nicely here for a time. I wonder if we have enough things with us . . ."

The duke had been quietly standing by, awaiting the outcome of this conversation. He could have offered to take charge of his friend's well-being, but something had made him refrain from making the offer. After all, Sir Frederick could use a woman's touch and it might prove interesting to have Satin within easy reach. He took his leave of Lady Jane and brushed Miss Bretton's hand. He said quietly, "I know Freddy will be in the best of good care with you hovering about him."

Miss Bretton smiled. "Which is more than I can count on in regards to my cousin's care in *your* company, your grace." It was said for his ears alone.

He gave her a sharp, considering look. "Perhaps you are wrong."

"Am I? I hope so," Miss Bretton returned.

Satin could not hear what they were saying to one another and felt a moment's twinge of jealousy. But she loved her cousin too much to allow this feeling to linger, so she immediately banished it and said lightly to the duke, "Must you leave? I rather thought you might take lunch with us?"

He smiled and offered her his arm. "Come then and do me the honor of walking me to my phaeton."

She took his arm and smiled up at him. Oh, faith, his eyes. His devilishly, exquisitely deep blue eyes sent such dreams into her head. "You won't stay then . . . ?"

"I regret . . . truly, that I cannot. Remember, I am promised to the squire and really must make some haste if I am not to insult the old gentleman."

"Oh, of course." Then wistfully, "Will I see you while we are staying here?"

He looked at her long and sighed. "You know, Satin, you should probably stay away from me."

"Yes, I know," she answered. "But I don't know that I can. Do you wish me to?"

He flicked her nose, then suddenly he was pulling her to the side of the building, hiding her from view and pushing her gently against the inn's outer wall, for he felt himself out of control. "No, Satin, I want you in my way, but I make you no promises beyond this." He was bending down, touching her lips with his own.

Her lips parted to receive his kiss and her hands went to his shoulders. She moved into his arms, and he held her tightly as one kiss moved into another, and she heard his voice, low, seductive and so very enticing.

"I want you, Satin . . ." His hand moved to the firmness of her small waist, then up to her breast.

She trembled at his touch, arched to his hard, lean body. What was she going to do? Could she make him love her? Would he love her if she gave him more of herself? This wasn't right. This was all wrong, for he wasn't speaking of love. This was something else, prompted only by desire, mutual desire, but *she* loved him—loved him!

She had to break away. This was going too far, his kisses were burning her into senselessness, his tongue was teasing her in a way she knew would soon have her out of control. She pulled out of his arms. He eased her back to him. She murmured something, she wasn't sure what.

He answered, "But you want me, too, Satin, you know you do. . . ."

She woke up. He did not love her. She had to conquer her emotions or she would be lost. "Stop it, Nick. This is no good. What you want . . . what I want, are two different things, and though I could go on letting you kiss me, touch me, for you do it so very expertly, I know better, for I would never be able to adhere to the rules of the game."

He pulled himself erect and looked into her dark eyes. Damn, but he wanted her and in a way that was more than physical; however, not enough to promise her marriage. No, not enough for that. He touched her nose and then her lips. "I am a cad, forgive me," he answered.

"And I am just as bad, for I know I teased you to it," she riposted with a smile. Her heart was breaking. She felt a constriction in her throat. He wouldn't see her again. She knew it. Oh, faith, she wanted to cry, but she held herself in check and allowed him to take his leave without another word. She stood for a long while and stared into space. There would never be anyone else whom she could love. There was nothing worthwhile any longer, and with a heart that was no longer the same, she turned and went back into the inn, for she wanted her room and she wanted to be alone.

Adam and Eve was the name of a tavern in Soho. It had a large galley with skittle alleys and cosy arbors designed in the seventeenth century. There were the remnants of a small pond that had for a time housed goldfish, but its landscaped court had long since gone to weed and ruin, as had its clientele. What had once been a tavern of social repute had become an inn frequented by persons of questionable character.

Through its weathered doors common women, pickpockets, footpads and highwaymen came and went. Thus it was a surprising thing to look within and find Sir Edward Danton in all his finery; but there he was at one of the round oak tables and with him was a young man dressed in what was surely the costume of an office clerk.

Sir Edward leaned back against the hardness of his wooden chair and drew on his cigar as he stared at the youthful clerk seated across the table from him. He had to think this out. What was this young man telling him?

"Are you certain you heard the young woman's name and that it was Waverly?"

"That's it. Oi 'eard it, oi did, and remember thinking what a fine little loidy she was. Oi liked 'er, oi did. Give me a smile when she passed. How could oi forget 'er name, but 'ere . . . you don't mean 'er 'arm, do ye?"

"Devil is in it that I don't. I should, for all she is putting me through, but rest easy. I don't mean her any harm," Sir Edward answered. "Besides, you didn't worry about that when you accepted the purse I gave you." A marked sneer crossed Sir Edward's face.

The youth felt his cheeks flood with hot color. This was humiliating, but it was the way of the world, his world. "As to that, oi ain't plump enough in the pocket to go throwing away the gold you offered, but loikes oi told ye, oi can't say fer sure t'was 'er who wrote that book. Could be anyone. Could be Byron 'imself. After all, was Lord Byron who was wit 'er." He shook his head. "Ole Murry he didn't trust anyone to draw up the contracts. He done them 'imself, even though oi've done a few now and then . . ."

"Which only proves the point," Sir Edward said softly and more to himself than to the clerk.

"Eh?" The boy screwed up his thin face. "What point might that be?"

"Never mind." Sir Edward got up from the table and looked around as though seeing the place for the first time. That he should be forced to such disagreeable surroundings was beyond belief. That he should be pushed to such backhanded measures was deeply troubling, but he was a man used to getting his own way and, at the moment, the method didn't matter as long as it served the end! He looked the boy over distastefully. "You will forget this meeting ever took place."

"That oi will. Need me job and wouldn't 'ave it if word got back to ole Murry that oi was talking . . . er . . . out of school."

Disdainfully, Sir Edward inclined his pomaded

head of chestnut curls and there deposited his beaver top hat at a rakish angle. Without a backward glance he left the clerk still seated at the table and made his way outdoors. Once outside he sucked in air and frowned again. This was what he wanted, Satin in his power, yet that he had to stoop to such means . . .

It was a blow to his pride. Here he was, Sir Edward Danton, the very pink of the pinkest! The power he had always wielded over society had not left him prepared for Satin's rejection. *She* had not prepared him for her rejection. She had flirted with him, audaciously tantalized him and given him reason to believe she was attracted to him. Her admiration had, in fact, spurred him on, had teased his desire and seduced his heart.

He realized sadly as he walked the avenue to where his coach was waiting that he wanted Satin to want him. He wanted to conquer her heart, to win her love, and wisely, all too wisely, he knew that that would never happen. Thus there was only one solution. This last one.

Satin should be in Brighton by now. He would travel there in the morning as his lodgings should be in readiness for him by then. He would have a message taken to her. Yes, she would comply. She would have no choice, but he would have to be careful. Satin was a rebellious chit. She might challenge him to expose her. He would have to word it so that she would think of her father, her aunt, her cousin. Indeed, he knew just what he would say.

Chapter Eleven

"Satin?" Miss Bretton cooed sweetly.

Satin knew she was in for a sharp setdown, but she bought the bait. "Yes?"

"Adone-do!" snapped her cousin. "I simply won't discuss this with you any further." Cory reached for the bedroom-door latch, but Satin stopped her by taking a step forward.

"Adone-do?" Satin repeated in dumbfounded resonance. "Adone-do? What, are we slipping into Shakespeare and medieval scenes? What can you mean, adone-do?"

"Enough. Enough is what I mean. You have asked me if I am forming a *tendre* for Sir Frederick. I have answered you. Now that is all there is. I like him—nothing more."

"Then why do you hover about him, watching to be sure he eats his meals and drinks that vile tisane you prepared for him yourself?"

"That vile tisane brought down his fever, didn't it?" Cory returned.

"Yes, but—"

"But that is precisely why I made certain he drink it. The sooner he recovers, the sooner we may all leave here," Miss Bretton answered her in frigid terms. "Now, stop badgering me."

"Cory?" Satin sighed and gave it up. She found she just wasn't able to play. "Right then, I won't have at you. Go on then . . . go do whatever it is you are itching to do."

Cory frowned. "Why don't you come with me? You don't mean to sit up here and sulk just because I didn't tell you what you wanted to hear?"

Satin's dark eyes flashed. "I don't mean to sulk just because you won't confide in me, no." She put her hand to stall the abuse Cory was about to fling at her. "But neither do I mean to sit with Sir Frederick just right now. I think—I think I'll just rest a bit."

"Rest? It is the middle of the morning," returned Cory. "Satin, what is it? What is wrong?"

"Nought. What could be wrong?"

"Now, who is not confiding in whom?" Cory returned.

"Go on, Cory. Sir Frederick may need you, and right now I think I'll just read . . . or something. Maybe I'll scribble some more nonsense for that new book I am developing." Satin looked away and then moved to the window seat.

Cory watched her a moment, then decided to let her cousin be for a while. Perhaps that was what Satin needed: to write and get her mind off all this nonsense about Sir Frederick.

Satin scooped up the skirt of her maize morning gown and propped her chin on her bent knees before her. It had only been two days since she had seen Wildfire, but it seemed an eternity. Two days! He had not even come by to visit Sir Frederick. He had sent along a message for his friend, a missive brought from the Bleinham Grange with the duke's crest on the seal, but there had been no word from him for her. Well, that, she supposed, was that.

She had been too free and easy with him. What did he want with such as she? He could have any woman he wanted. He had had sophisticated belles like Julia Hartly who knew the rules of the game and didn't pout to play them. Well, she couldn't just sit in window seats looking over empty courtyards and wish she was elsewhere, now could she? What to do?

She had to bring her spirits up. Ride? Hmmm, perhaps. Yes, perhaps she might see him . . .

Satin! she chided herself. Stop it. You must not think that way. No, then, no ride. Yes, but . . . She was already on her feet, throwing off her morning gown and reaching for her riding habit. "But" was not a strong enough word to stop her, and she certainly was not going to argue with her heart. Her heart? It cried, it demanded, it pleaded for free rein, and in order to give it free rein, she had to get on her horse!

Lord Wildfire was in the devil of a mood! What was he doing daydreaming about a chit of a girl? Absurd. He could have any woman he wanted, when he wanted . . . right? So what then was he doing? Satin, with her impish smile and her dark eyes so full of promise. Satin, with her taunting laugh and her challenge to touch. Satin.

Enough! Two days had passed, and he had kept away. He had even avoided visiting Sir Frederick. The squire had invited guests to the grange and had attempted to keep the duke occupied with various entertainments, yet the young duke was scarcely able to give the assembled company a smile, let alone his attention.

What was wrong with him? He didn't like losing control of himself, and here he was, caught by a passion he didn't understand and couldn't contain. Time. It didn't need anything more than time. What was it that they once told him so long ago when he had been disappointed in a woman, "Time heals all wounds of the heart and opens the eyes. What we think was, is, no longer, and what we want can be put aside."

Satin. So he would put aside his desire for Satin. He sighed out loud, heard himself and sighed again. The thing of it was that he had his eyes open, wide open, and they were filled with her. She tickled his imagination. She lit something inside him he had thought beyond reach. She touched him with softness, rattled him with her ferocious vitality, liberated a hunger in him with her open smile and—and this was all absurd!

He called a servant with the bellrope and ordered his horse to be brought round to him. Damn, if he wouldn't visit with Sir Frederick. After all, Freddy was a friend and he wasn't going to allow a chit of a girl to keep him away . . . no, indeed! Frightened of Satin? Nonsense. He could handle his feelings for the wench. Damn, if he couldn't!

Satin was in a state of depression, but as she took the fence flying, her short black curls whipped by the wind, she felt some of her spirits lift. This was what she needed, a gallop across the fields. A light drizzle had started, and she felt the mist touch her cheeks and dampen her uncovered curls. How foolish to have gone out without her hat and cloak. Her father and aunt were visiting friends in the vicinity and had not been there to stop her when she stormed out of the inn and hopped on her gelding bareback. With a grimace and a rueful smile she almost wished they had been there to stop her as she was damned uncomfortable, for her horse's withers was just a bit too high.

Then suddenly her horse snorted with an exclamation of surprise and fear, for he had found a chuckhole. In an instant he was tumbling to the ground and sending her flying off his back as he went down. Satin hit the turf hard, and, as she rolled, her head met a rock, which grazed and stunned her. She felt herself slipping into a dark void and knew that if she didn't get a hold of her senses she would blank out. *Stars!* Everywhere there were stars and they split and illuminated the blackness with streaks of light. And then there was nothing.

The duke sat his horse and watched as Satin managed to take the fence and remain seated. He pulled a face, for she had not done it with the greatest of

style, then realized that she had no saddle! Damn,
the chit was hare-brained. What was wrong with
her? Certes! She was riding across the field—and
then he saw her horse go down. Something inside of
him reacted in a way he had never experienced before, but there was no time for that. He clucked to his
horse and was after her in a moment, but even as he
approached he saw that she was not moving, and it
very nearly stopped the beating of his heart!

He was off his horse in a thrice and down on one
knee, taking up her shoulders and calling her name,
"Satin! Satin!"

Through the blackness she heard him and smiled.
It was so very pleasant, his voice, saying her name.
Perhaps if she just kept her eyes closed, she might go
on hearing his voice . . . So, very naturally, she kept
her eyes closed.

He attempted to maintain his composure and
think of what next to do. All he was able to accom-
plish in this vein was the repetition of her name.
"Satin?" he called again, this time even more desperately.

She opened her eyes. Her lids fluttered, and her
dark eyes centered on his worried expression. She
studied him for a long moment before managing to
say, "Oh, hello."

He laughed. Absurdly, he laughed and hugged her
to him before setting her away again and taking on a
stern expression. "What the devil do you mean coming out here on an untacked horse and taking an un-
familiar field at such a pace?"

She remembered. She had had a fall, and, with a
startled exclamation, she attempted to move and
look to her animal. "My horse?" was what she answered.

"He is here, grazing, and appears to have sustained no injury . . . little thanks to his mistress."

Her lips moved into a pout, but she admitted,
"Yes, I suppose you are right." With that she real-

ized that she was cradled in his arms and once again attempted to move. He held her fast, and she looked at his face and said quietly, "I think I can get up now."

Gently, he released her, got to his feet and gave her his hand, helping her to rise. She swayed and he steadied her.

"Satin," he said softly, "are you sure you haven't done yourself an injury?"

She smiled ruefully. "I am quite sure I have, but only to my pride."

He flicked her nose. "It would take more than a tumble from your horse to daunt *your* pride!" It was meant to tease, to rouse her, to bring the color back into her cheeks.

It worked quite nicely. Her hands went to her hips, and her dark eyes flashed. "What is that supposed to mean?"

"Why, Lady Satin, I don't think that is quite the stance your Aunt Jane would approve of," he teased her further.

"She would if she knew you had provoked it," Satin threw at him. Then tenaciously, "So answer me, your grace. What did you mean about my pride?"

He laughed. "Nought. I only wanted to see you react." He reached for her hand and dropped a light kiss on her gloved knuckles. "Come on then, I'll hoist you up on my horse and we'll take yours in tow."

She stood fast, her hand still held in his. "No, I will not do that."

His brow went up. "Won't you?"

She shook her head. "That would be terribly uncomfortable. I know 'tis most romantic to do so and one always reads about knights charging about on their horses taking up damsels in distress, but this particular damsel does not mean to squeeze on to a saddle with you. . . ."

"Hmmm." He was amused. "I see your point and

think I have the solution. We shall both slide on to your gelding and take my horse in tow since your horse does not sport a saddle."

A frowned flickered across her face. This was still not to her liking. "I really don't think that is necessary . . ." she started to protest and found herself scooped cradlelike in his arms. As he carried her the distance to her grazing horse, she attempted to chastize him. "Your grace!" she said austerely, and when he would only smirk, "Nicholas! Put me down this instant . . ." And when he still only seemed to smile bovinely: "Nick! Put me down . . . *Nick!*"

In answer to all this he said, "I do so like the way you say my name in all its varying forms. There are a few more. Would you like to try them?" With that he deposited her atop her grazing gelding. As this caused the horse to step forward onto its reins, they had a moment where the duke attempted to right the situation and Satin held on to the horse's mane. This accomplished, she slid her legs round the animal's flanks and found that the duke was as agile as he was handsome. It took scarcely a bounce and he was up and astride behind her on the horse. One arm held her tight, the other had the reins as he urged the horse forward and took up the reins of his own horse. These he put into Satin's hands.

"I am afraid we shall have to take the long way round the field and avoid the fences, unless you wish me to try them while we are riding double?" He bantered.

"Hmmm. I wonder if that is possible," she mused.

He took her seriously. "Satin! You are incorrigible."

She laughed. "Clunch! I was only teasing."

His grace had never before been called a clunch or anything like it, especially by a green girl. He was taken aback. She realized this, and it renewed her mirth.

He eyed her profile as she laughed, and it occurred

to him that he never seemed to feel quite as strongly as he did when he was in her company. Everything else seemed to slip into the background. All his senses came to life. She drew on his sense of humor, on his temper, softening it, gentling it so that he would see things in a new light. Why? What was it about her that did this to him? Yes, he was attracted by her dark eyes, her dusky curls, her lively mannerisms, her cherry lips. Yes, he wanted her body; yes, he wanted her. . . . But there was something different about this situation and he had to rid himself of it. He just had to, but later—later when she wasn't so very near . . .

"Satin?" he said softly as her laughter subsided.

"Y-es?" she returned, moving to look at his face, then slid quickly back into position again as her move brought his hand closer to her breast. She felt herself flush as she became aware of his nearness.

"Can you deny the attraction we have for one another?" he asked quietly, and then demanded of himself, what the deuce was he doing?

"No," she answered honestly, surprising herself with her admission. "But what does that mean? You want no ties, and I think I would be happier going on just as I am. I don't believe in knights in shining armor. Behind the armor is flesh and blood with all its weaknesses, so don't think I am in waiting for the impossible man. I am not."

"Then why deny us our time together?" What was he doing? Was he seducing this virgin? Damnation, that was just what he was doing, but she was teasing it out of him.

She was glad that she couldn't look at him. She wanted to punch him, but she maintained her composure. "Am *I* doing that? I rather thought my name and what I owe my family and my reputation did it for me."

"I see," he returned softly. "Of course, you are quite right." He kissed the nape of her neck.

She felt a tingle of excitement ripple through her, and for fun she moved her curls away from her neck and laughed. "Here, you missed a spot. . . ."

He laughed out loud and found himself hugging her tightly and dropping several kisses on her neck. "Ye gods, but I could be forced to the altar for doing this to you in public!"

"Then, by all means, stop at once!" she returned, a smile in her eyes and her lips curving.

It struck him that he might enjoy having this little minx for a wife. Marriage? Egad! What was he thinking! What would it serve him? Trouble. Only trouble. He wasn't marrying anyone, especially this little she-devil!

Chapter Twelve

Sir Edward had hired bachelor lodgings for the Brighton season. They were centrally located, decorated in the first stare of elegance and furnished with more style and flare than comfort. This singular thought came to mind as he attempted to find some measure of ease in a wing chair situated by the bow window, which overlooked the quiet street below.

He sighed and came to grips with himself. This was utterly frustrating, but in the end the Waverlys would arrive. After all, where could they be? They had taken a house and that house was already staffed; therefore Satin was on her way—wasn't she? He stood and paced over the Oriental carpet. This was getting to be an obsession. Why not give it up? Why not give her up? What did he want with a madcap woman? What did he want with Satin? What, indeed?

She had denied herself to him. So be it. Famous. He could not, would not, be beaten. Besides, she needed a setdown! And he was just the man to give it to her, wasn't he? Damn, if he wasn't. Ah, he could see his man taking the steps of his lodgings. Right, then. He stood, his hands clasped at his back as he waited for the study door to open and his man to enter.

"Sir?" His gentleman's gentleman was breathless. Sir Edward was a generous employer and could be counted on to toss an additional coin now and then for a service well done.

"Well, what have you found out? Have they arrived yet?" Sir Edward was impatient for the news and was scarcely able to contain himself in his usual style of placidity.

"No, the earl and his family have not arrived, but I spoke with their housekeeper and she says they had word from them last night." He paused for breath. "The Waverlys are putting up at an inn near Bleinham Grange just ten miles north. They don't expect to leave there before the week is out. Somethin' about a sick friend they found on the road . . ."

"What in thunder? What sick friend?" Sir Edward was frowning.

"She didn't say, sir."

Sir Edward dismissed him and took to pacing. What was this new development? He couldn't take the delay. It just didn't fit in with the frenzy his plans had created in his mind. Once again he summoned his valet. This time, however, he gave the order for his open phaeton to be brought round and his overnight portmanteau to be prepared. He would find this inn and Lady Satin and then—and then he would make Satin see she was meant for no other man. Indeed, he meant to take fine advantage of Satin in any way he could, but first, damn it all, first he had to get to her!

* * *

Sir Frederick looked across at his pacing friend and grinned. "Shall I tell you what is wrong with you, Wildfire, old fellow?"

"Go to hell." The duke smiled sweetly at him.

"I might do that . . . then again, who knows, methinks I might yet be saved." He thought of Cory's soft hazel eyes and grew serious all at once, saw that his friend was studying him and smiled again. "As you might yet be."

"Me? No chance of that. I sold my soul long ago. . . ."

"No, you never did that, Nick. It was wrenched from you against your will when you were too young and too green to know how to fight back."

"It doesn't matter how I lost it; the fact is it's no longer in my keeping." The duke sat on the edge of Sir Frederick's bed. "So what ails you, Freddy? You look well enough to me."

"I am well enough. What ails me? Love, old boy, love. Don't mean to leave this place till I have it well in hand."

"Oh? And is there a chance of that, do you think?" The duke was eyeing his friend in some surprise.

"Don't know. She seems to think more of me today than she did yesterday. Perhaps she will think more of me tomorrow than she does today."

"Really? Satin gave me no indication that you two had become such great friends." He was on his feet again, eyeing his friend frostily.

Sir Frederick looked askance at him for a long moment before understanding dawned. "Satin?" He released a short laugh. "Good God, man, you do have it bad! Did I say anything about Satin? I was referring to myself and Miss Bretton."

"Miss Bretton?" returned the duke, and then more brightly, "Of course, Miss Bretton." He sat down again and gave his friend's thigh a comrade's squeeze. "Do you mean to come up to scratch, Freddy, tie the knot and settle down?" He shook his head. "Would never have believed it of you."

Sir Frederick laughed. "Indeed, I am finding it rather hard to believe myself, but that's what I intend, if she will have me."

The duke snorted. "And why wouldn't she?"

Sir Frederick's face clouded over. "I haven't told her yet . . ."

"Told her?" Then he remembered and snapped his

fingers in the air. "That old tale! It's dead and buried, leave it be."

"Can't. She must know. I don't want her to hear rumors about me and not understand the facts . . . but after she hears, she might not want me."

"Nonsense. Miss Bretton is a broth of a woman. She'll stand buff—if she loves you. Does she, do you think? I can't imagine why she should!" He dodged the pillow that was flung at his head.

A knock sounded at the door and Sir Frederick called admittance. Miss Bretton appeared, and the duke could not help but notice the transformation that came over his friend's features. Love. It was all too apparent that his friend was certainly in the throes of deep emotion. Love? Bah! What did it mean? Nought. A fleeting thing that discomforted a man until he was no longer able to think for himself. Love, indeed!

A moment later he was taking his leave and making his way out of the inn. He had no intention of seeking Lady Satin out. He had left her more than an hour ago and . . . Then he heard the sound of her laughter. He forgot himself for a moment and turned in the direction of the sound. She stood at the side of the barn, teasing some youth about some frivolity. The duke frowned, Her manners were far too easy. What the devil could she be conversing about with a stable boy? He raised his hand and silently mouthed a good-bye as she looked his way, but she halted him by moving towards him and stopping him just inside the stable door.

"Oh, are you leaving already?" she asked, a touch of disappointment purposely inflected in her voice. She had carefully washed and changed into a summer gown of yellow muslin. Her dark curls were in a mass profusion round her heart-shaped face and her dark eyes stroked him as she spoke.

"I am afraid so. I am expected at the grange," he returned lamely.

She smiled sweetly, putting aside the ride they had just shared, putting aside his teasing, his touch, the feel of his kisses on the back of her neck. Somehow she had to make him want her; she extended her ungloved hand to him. "Good-bye then. Perhaps I shall see you in Brighton?"

He took up her hand and dropped a perfunctory kiss upon her fingers. Blue eyes met dark and held. It was a moment charged with feelings he was not about to admit to himself and certainly not to her. "Perhaps, though, we should not."

She inclined her head. "Whatever you think best. For my part, I shall miss you if we do not again meet." Was this wise? Was she doing the right thing?

She was an amazing female. What was she doing now? He pulled her to him by the hand he still held and, quickly glancing round the barn to make certain that they were alone, he took her into his arms. His mouth closed on hers, his lips gently parted her own and his tongue found its way, teasing a response from her.

She pressed herself against his hard, lean body, and her hands went to his shoulders. His kiss moved into another and yet another until he was gently, deftly pressing his lips to her ear. "Satin, this is what will happen if we continue to meet, and as I have no wish to hurt you and don't mean to wed anyone, we had better say good-bye."

It hurt. She was at a loss. What to do? How could she win this man for her own? She allowed instinct to take over. "You are right, of course." She sighed and gently eased out of his embrace. She turned and started out of the barn, but as she got to the door, she stopped, giggled and threw over her shoulder, "Dearest Wildfire, allow me to say, however, that if ever I decide to play with fire, I shall come to you."

A moment later she was gone. He stood. Dark eyes twinkled in his mind. The feel of her body tingled his nerve endings and stirred his manhood into longing.

Marriage? Not he! Marriage, to an unruly minx with a wayward spirit . . . and such dark, laughing eyes. . . .

Sir Edward stared as the duke spurred his horse over a fence and took the shortcut to his host's estate. What in blazes was Wildfire doing here? Sir Edward's hazel eyes narrowed with his thoughts. Could Wildfire himself be seriously interested in Lady Satin? He knew, of course, that the duke had displayed a marked degree of attention in Satin's direction, but he had assumed (as did most of the haut ton) that it meant nothing. However, the duke's presence here, attending Lady Satin in the wilds of Sussex, meant something indeed.

Here was the King of Rakehells, the Prince of Flirts (Wildfire was noted for these titles), paying court to Lady Satin. So that was it. Lady Satin had spurned him in favor of the duke. Of course. Why had he not seen that? There was even something to forgive in such a decision. Forgive her, yes, but release her, no. He still meant to have her—one way or another.

He drove his pair of bays into the inn's courtyard and nimbly jumped down from his seat to hand over the driving reins to the groom who had hurried out of the carriage house. He then reset his top hat rakishly angled over his well-shaped brows, brushed off a speck of lint from his dark brown cutaway coat and eyed his Hessians. Satisfied with his appearance, he made his way into the inn.

There he was pleased enough to run right into Satin, who was rounding the corner and throwing a jest to her aunt over her shoulder. She collided against Sir Edward's chest and put out her hand with an exclamation, "Oooh! I *am* sorry . . ." And then seeing who it was, "Why, Sir Edward!"

He held her shoulders to steady her, and his smile was at first quite genuine, for she felt small and well formed in his hands. "Just the lady I wished to see," he answered.

"But this is a surprise." She was too astounded to say more.

"I looked for you in Brighton and your housekeeper informed me that some trouble kept you here. I came at once to see if I could be of some assistance."

"Who is that?" called Lady Jane, taking up her walking stick and peeping round the bend. "Well, well, Sir Edward," was what she said, her composure still intact.

He went forward and took up the hand she allowed him; they passed a quiet greeting before she eyed him speculatively.

"No doubt you are here to visit with my niece, so if you like I will ring for tea for you both. I have already enjoyed a cup and think I will go and bother my brother to entertain me with a game of cards."

Satin wanted to call her back. Why was Aunt Jane doing this? Aunt Jane didn't even care for Sir Edward. Why leave her alone with him? "Auntie . . ." She did in fact call her back.

Her aunt stopped and turned. "Yes, love?"

"I really don't want any tea . . ." She turned to Sir Edward. "Perhaps you would like something stronger with my papa?"

"You are too kind, but in fact what I would like is a stroll around the lovely gardens I happened to notice on my way into the courtyard." He smiled at Lady Jane. "Would you care to join us, my lady?"

Lady Jane waved her walking stick. "Very nicely executed, sir; however, I don't think it will do you an ounce of good. No, you don't see that, do you? Never mind. I don't mean to play duenna for you in this instance." She released a short snort. "Truth is, Satin don't need one." So saying, she was off. To her mind, Sir Edward had come to propose. He had informed the earl of his intentions some time ago and the earl had gladly agreed to the match. Might as well allow the man to get it over with. He wasn't the man for Satin. She knew it, Satin knew it and it was time Sir Edward was informed of it. She had no way of knowing the course Sir Edward was taking in order to attain his goal.

Satin watched her go and felt uneasy about being left alone with Sir Edward. There was something about him that frightened her. She smiled and inclined her head. "Sir Edward—"

He interrupted her. "Ned. Do call me Ned. It is what all my intimates call me."

"Ned, then. I think I know why you wish to be private with me and I . . . I really don't think—"

He interrupted her again, "Satin, there is something I must say to you. Allow me that opportunity."

She took a long drag of air. "And shall I be safe in your company . . . out in the gardens?"

He laughed. "You are safe in no red-blooded man's company. However, if you think I may lay hands on you, rest easy. I shan't."

Trustingly, she smiled at him and nearly disarmed him in that moment. Nearly, but not quite. He bent his arm for her and she laid her ungloved hand upon it, and for the space of a few moments she allowed him to chatter idly about town affairs until they were well into the landscaping of the rose garden. Sir Edward was shaking his head over the Prince Regent's latest scandal.

"His reign will end in insanity, like his father before him. Satin, when one considers all that he does, it is almost too farcical to uphold him as more than a madman."

She nodded. "Particularly when one considers how he flits from Tory to Whig, but politics is not what you mean to discuss with me, sir?" She eyed him quizzically.

"Always ready to rush head-on into everything, Satin? Neck-or-nothing paces may end in hurting you, child."

"I didn't know that directness was considered a neck-or-nothing pace," she answered him, her dark eyes taking on a militant light.

He laughed. "That is because you lack experience and sagacity."

"Oh, really?" She had her chin up, and her eyes were sparkling.

"Allow me to illustrate," he returned. "*Passion's Seed.* An interesting title, don't you think?"

"Interesting? No. Explicit, yes," she answered easily, yet she felt a wariness take hold of her spine.

"Intriguing as well." He went on, "In one chapter our author tells us, 'any woman can make a man fall in love with her; but, ah, the woman who can keep him so!' What do you say, penned by female or male?" He looked into her dark eyes and was confirmed in his conclusions.

"The author is a male. At least Felix Gamble has the ring of a man's name."

"Hmmm. Perhaps." Then as though he just remembered an incident, he asked, "Do you recall Lady Jersey's weekend affair last year at Middleton? Of course you must. It was when Holland made a gross fool of himself and took a dive into the goldfish pond."

She knew what he was driving at. Ye gods. Why had she put that incident into her book? She had disguised it, changed the scenery, changed the style, but . . . What was Sir Edward getting at? She knew. Something inside shouted at her, something inside said: Sir Edward knows. He knows. "Yes, I remember." She attempted to smile.

"Hmmm. I rather thought you did, *my lady Felix,*" he said softly.

She looked at him. There was no one about. "Sir Edward, you don't realize what you are saying. I could cause you no end of trouble if you attempt to slander me." She took the bull by the horn.

He lifted his brow and nailed her. "I don't think so,

my love. You see, I have the proof. I have a copy of the contract you signed. Don't think that because you dealt with Murry directly that you are safe. There is always someone who needs money badly enough to play the spy."

She closed her eyes. Her world seemed to swim round in her head for a moment and then she shoved such weakness away. Right then. He had made it his business to find out about her. Why?

"What—what made you suspect me?" she managed to ask.

"The style of the story, my dear. There were times when I was reading and I could very nearly hear you rattling off some anecdote, and then your father was in deep debt, but suddenly he was not. He had not come into an inheritance, and I made it my business to find out that he had not secured any great sum at the gaming tables. I knew that you enjoyed scribbling. You had done a few pieces in the past for various papers . . ."

She put up her chin. "Right then. So you know."

"Ask me what I want for my silence."

"For your silence you remain the gentleman I have always thought you," she returned sharply.

He laughed without mirth. "Oh, no, honor in this instance means nought to me. You, Satin. I want *you*."

She sucked in air. "*Me?* You want me? I may have scribbled out a novel, my buck, but I am not some wench you can call to your bed with such a threat!"

He laughed again, but this time he was amused. "Don't mistake me. Satin, I want you as my wife."

She stopped herself from answering immediately. She was angry. She was cornered, but she had to take care. She looked at him speculatively. "Sir Edward, tell me you want a woman you must buy? Is that the sort of life you wish to begin with a bride? I thought you had more pride than that." She had said this to him carefully, hoping to shame him out of his intentions.

He was too smart for her. "I cannot be manipulated with words, my dear. I want you any way I can get you. Once you are mine, you will learn to please me and, in the end, will be pleased yourself."

"No. I won't marry you."

"Then I will destroy you and your father."

"I can't believe that." She put her hand on his arm. "Sir Edward, I couldn't be wrong about you. I liked you. I really liked you . . ."

"Then marry me, girl, and make us both happy."

"I can't do that. I—I am in love with someone else . . ."

"Ah, I was forgetting the Duke of Morland."

She gasped. "I didn't say . . ."

"You didn't have to. I really must groom you to understand that my experiences have taught me a great deal." He took her chin. "Do you think he will want you when he has learned you are the author of a novel considered by most of the ton to be on the border of risqué?"

She looked at her toes. "He doesn't know that and he still doesn't want me."

"Doesn't he? More fool, he," Sir Edward answered. "But I do want you and, Satin, I mean to have you."

Time, what she needed was time. She frowned up at him and her hands worked one another agitatedly. "Sir Edward, I don't want my father hurt by all this. He had expressly forbidden me from publishing and I went ahead against his wishes. Is there no chance that you would reconsider your decision?"

"Satin, the sooner you are my bride, the better it will be for you, for your father and, my dear, for me." He traced the outline of her lips with his finger and said on a low note, "I want you, Satin. Do you hear me?"

"Yes, yes, I hear you, but I am unwilling . . . Do you want an unwilling bride?"

"If that bride is you," he returned coldly.

"Then . . . at least give me some months to get used to the notion."

He chortled over this request. "No."

She touched his arm. "Ned, if you want me, really want me, and I have no choice in this matter, at least honor me with a few weeks' courtship."

"You have had that and you refused my suit."

"I—I had hopes . . ." she started.

"Of Lord Wildfire," he answered, frowning. "Indeed, I think the King of Rakehells has led you a dance in that quarter." He looked at her. "Right then, I shall give you a few days' time before I send in the announcement of our engagement to the newspapers."

"A few days? You mean to woo me in a few days?" She was still attempting to coax more time out of him.

He nearly sneered, for he felt himself the victor and with the power came a sense of superiority and a dash of cruelty. "My dearest child, I don't mean to woo you at all. I mean to take you."

Her dark eyes surveyed him coldly. "Do you know, Sir Edward, that a man obsessed does not always find satisfaction in the winning. I have it on good authority that when Leander swam the Hellespont, he was a man driven by true love's hottest blood, but having gone the distance, he was unable to make the girl!" She had shocked him and, taking the moment, tried to escape.

He reached out and held her arm in his firm grip. His answer was to bend and take her lips, and though he found them soft, though he found her mouth sweet, he found that she was not pliable. He set her aside and eyed her angrily.

"When I am done, Satin, your lips will part for mine and you will whisper my name against my ear."

"No, Sir Edward. I will not. You take by force that which can never be yours."

His brow moved, and his eyes were slits of fury. "We shall see." He released her arm. "In the meantime, you will inform the duke that you intend to become my bride and that he is no longer welcome at your side."

"No. I won't do that." She was near to tears, but she wouldn't let him see that.

"Won't you, my love? Then perhaps I shall." He started to move off.

"Sir Edward, please, it is not necessary. He has no wish to marry me . . ."

"Then you will not distress him by telling him you are promised to me."

She lowered her eyes. Quick, she told herself, what to do? There was a fire in Satin. She would not easily surrender. She did not now. "Sir Edward," she answered calmly, "if it is your wish that the duke be told such news, then, yes, you tell him!"

He was taken aback. He would have preferred that she take care of it. He wanted the duke to believe it, and he wasn't sure the duke would believe it from him. However, he could see she would be pushed no further. He inclined his head.

"It will give me the greatest of pleasure to inform Lord Wildfire he has lost you to me."

She had to have the last word in this. Such was her nature. "Sir Edward, he hasn't lost me, and you will never have me, not really." It was softly said and her message was clear, all too clear.

He fired up but controlled himself. "No? We shall see, for this first round has gone to me, as will all the others in the end."

She watched him go and leaned back against the oak tree for support. She wanted to cry, but what good would that do? She needed a clear head. Her world was falling apart all around her and there was nothing she could do to stop it if she didn't hold strong. There had to be an answer and she had to find it, somehow!

Chapter Thirteen

Cory gazed at Sir Frederick for a long moment. There was something in the recesses of his vague blue eyes that pulled at her heart. There was something in the gentleness of his smile that called a response from her. There was a naughty mischief lurking in his head, dancing round his words, that captured her imagination, and she knew she had fallen in love with him. However, she had to be cautious. He had just this moment recited a bit of pretty fluff to her, but he had not sounded sincere. She tapped his nose with her forefinger.

"Nonsense," she answered him. "I haven't the slightest notion what it means and what you mean by it."

"Don't, Cory," he replied gravely. "Not you. I thought of all the women in the world, you would always be honest with me."

She was surprised. "But I am being honest with you, Frederick. I don't know what you mean. You tell me 'there is a heaven in my eyes.' Well, that is very pretty, but what exactly do you mean?"

He looked at her sharply for a split second, then burst into laughter. He was sitting up in bed, but he reached for her hand and held it to his heart. "You are a treasure of wisdom." Then suddenly he released her hand. "And I am a cad to say such things to you."

"Are you? Why? Do you mean to bring me low?" She smiled at him.

He looked at her thoughtfully. "What do you know about me, Cory?"

"What should I know? You are a complex man with a gentle, kind and oddly mixed personality of contradictions. You are charming, you are good fun and . . . I like you a great deal."

"But you know nothing about me, and I am not fit to have your friendship," he said on a bitter note.

"Why?" Cory always dealt in directness.

"Have you never heard about me—about the scandal I raked over my name two years ago?" he answered, his eyes searching her face.

"I heard that you were involved in something that caused you a great deal of unhappiness and that you retired to your country home to weather the storm." She smiled sweetly at him. "Isn't the storm over yet, Frederick?"

He shook his head sadly. "Perhaps, but its ravages may yet return to haunt me and—and the woman who would carry my name."

She moved away from the bed and sat on the window seat. She didn't look at him, and he called her name.

"Cory . . . Cory . . . look at me."

She did. "What do you want me to answer to that statement? Freddy, we are friends. That is all that time has given us."

"I know, but, Cory, I am falling in love with you." It was simply said, but he was already rising out of the bed, taking the two long strides to her side, taking her hands and bringing her to her feet. "Cory?" Gently, he bent his head and dropped a soft kiss experimentally on her lips. Finding no resistance, his kiss lingered into yet another until she was held in his embrace and was breathing his name.

He set her aside. "I am a fiend."

"Are you?" she riposted, smiling up at him. "Why? Are your intentions dishonorable?"

He laughed. "You are a devil of a woman, and I

can see that you will forever have me at point non-plus. No, indeed, my intentions are most honorable, Miss Bretton, but first you must hear what all of London knows. . . ."

She shook her head. "No, not just this moment . . ." With that she put her arms around his neck and attempted to exhibit to him what she did want at that precise moment!

Sir Edward sent in his card at the Bleinham Grange and was taken in to the library to await the Duke of Morland. Here refreshment was served to him while he paced in front of the lead-paned glass doors. He stopped a moment, sipped his brandy and considered the long stretch of rolling green lawns. How, just how, was he going to handle this? He had ascertained the duke's direction from Lady Jane on his way out of the inn. The old squire was a notable power and he had no wish to antagonize anyone in the squire's household, nor did he want the duke as an enemy. He would have to wield a delicate hand in all of this.

The double doors of the library opened and the Duke of Morland entered. Sir Edward was struck by the electricity of the man before him, and as they shook hands in greeting, both were on their guard.

"So, Ned . . . what brings you here?"

"That is coming to the point," Sir Edward drolled pleasantly.

The duke grinned. "Yes, I think one or two of my intimates have told me I am sadly lacking in the graces."

Sir Edward moved to a leather-bound wing chair. "Perhaps we should sit down . . . ?"

"Certes, man, what can I have done?" This was from the duke who was grinning broadly but was acutely on his guard. He moved to the large, ornate and quite gothic desk, leaned back against it and folded his well-formed arms.

"The matter I am about to discuss with you concerns a lady," Sir Edward said on a low, grave note. It was artfully performed.

"Ah, of course, but damn it, Ned, you've never been in the petticoat line and I'd swear I haven't traversed your territory."

"Haven't you?" Sir Edward stood up and put his hands at his back. "Well, perhaps I should explain. You see, you are quite correct. I am not in the petticoat line; however, while you have only been playing with the lady in question, I have been in earnest."

True to his nickname, hot blood surged through the duke's veins. All at once he was supremely irritated. "Get to the point, Ned. I am not noted for patience."

"I am speaking of Lady Satin. She has this afternoon done me the honor of accepting my suit. I look forward to making her my wife in the very near future."

It hit the duke between the eyes. It plunged through his heart and pierced his soul. It hammered a wedge between all logical thoughts and it drew out his fury as nothing else could have at that moment in time. Satin had accepted Sir Edward? Impossible. Here was yet another woman capable of duplicity . . . but that wasn't quite fair. He couldn't really accuse her of that. She had the right to make a life for herself . . . but Sir Edward? He didn't have the right to feel what he was feeling. He shouldn't want to kill Sir Edward, to watch him bleed, but that was what he wanted just then. He said instead, "I felicitate you. How did you manage to bring this about?"

"Indeed you may wonder. We had something of a dispute, as I know you are aware of, that evening at the Rutledge Ball when you came upon us, but our separation has made us both realize that ours is a love match meant to be." Sir Edward knew what he was saying, what he was doing.

Wildfire's fists clenched inside the folds of his

arms. He didn't believe what he was hearing. It couldn't be true. Not Satin and Edward. Not Satin and anyone else but himself. Hadn't he just touched her, held her in his arms? Hadn't she responded?

"One wonders how you knew where Lady Satin was, as her stay at the Red Hart was by the veriest chance . . . ?" the duke questioned.

"A note was sent round to me in Brighton." Sir Edward lied so well.

It cut through the duke sharply, painfully. He inclined his head. "Well, again, my congratulations. She will, I think, lead you a lively dance, but one that you, as any man would, will enjoy." He took a moment to collect himself and then added quietly, "But, and don't misunderstand me, Ned, for I am pleased enough you chose to share your wonderful news with me, I am puzzled. Why go out of your way to do so?"

Sir Edward smiled, putting on a fine face. "One could not help but note your interest in my Lady Satin these past weeks, and today as I rode to the inn, I noticed you riding off and assumed you had been visiting with Satin."

The duke cut him off. "You assumed? Satin did not mention it to you?"

"I think we were so involved with other matters that it slipped her mind," Sir Edward answered. He drained the remaining contents of his glass and set it down on the side table.

"I see," the duke returned quietly, thoughtfully, for, in truth, he did not see, not at all. What was all this? How had Satin accepted Ned's suit? He had heard her reject him. With his own ears he had heard Satin reject Sir Edward. Right then, so what was this?

"Therefore, under the circumstances, I felt it incumbent upon myself to present the news to you."

"Did you? That is what I don't understand. I would have read your news in the papers . . ."

"No. We do not plan on putting in the announcement of our engagement for another ten days or so."

"Really? Odd that. If Satin had decided to be mine, I would be shouting it from the rooftops," returned the duke. Now why had he said that? To goad Edward on? Yes, but why? Because, damn it, something was wrong!

"As to that, we thought Satin would be more comfortable receiving congratulations from our various friends when she is installed in her Brighton home," Sir Edward answered glibly.

The duke eyed him. Nothing rang true. Satin and Sir Edward? Perhaps, yet would Satin go directly into Ned's arms? Only hours ago she . . . Bah! He was well rid of her! Sir Edward was good ton, and if any woman could wield him, Satin could! He raised his own still-full glass of brandy. "I salute you your conquest and wish you all the happiness in the world." Why the devil didn't his words sound sincere? Even to his own ears, he sounded false.

Chapter Fourteen

"Tell Aunt Jane!" Cory did not usually stamp her foot when provoked, but she found herself doing so now. She would not allow Satin to throw her life away. She did not see a solution out of the problem, but she was very certain Lady Jane with all her vast experiences might.

"No! How can I?" Satin wailed. "She would feel it her duty to tell Papa, who would forbid the marriage and take on society full score—and be ruined because of me."

"Satin, think! You cannot marry Sir Edward. You do not love him . . ."

"Love? What is love? He is attractive and at one time I did think of him romantically," countered Satin.

"And then along came Lord Wildfire," returned Cory sharply. "So tell me, can you allow Sir Edward to hold you, kiss you, touch you, Satin? Can you allow it?"

"Mercy." Satin was near tears. "You do have a way of bringing it home, don't you?" She took to pacing the floor of the room she and her cousin shared. Nick, she thought, if only Nick could save me . . . Save me? Why should he? He will thank the gods he is well out of my sphere.

A knock sounded at their door. Cory eyed her cousin. "Are you all right?" she whispered.

Satin nodded and called out herself, "Y-es?"

The door opened, and Lady Jane put in her head.

"Your father wants me to advise you that we leave for Brighton in the morning. He will brook no arguments. He was with Sir Frederick earlier, and both of them feel the short trip will do him no harm. After all, his arm is set and he no longer seems susceptible to fever."

"But his carriage. . ." objected Cory.

"They brought it round a little while ago," returned Lady Jane, eyeing her niece, then adding, "Corine, it would appear you and I have something to discuss, and though I don't mean to bother you about it just yet, when we are comfortable in Brighton we shall get to it."

"Yes, Aunt Jane," returned Miss Bretton carefully.

The look Lady Jane cast her nieces was speculative. Something was afoot. She was no fool, but she wasn't about to intrude on their privacy. She would give them just enough free rein and hope they wouldn't fall. After all, they were sensible girls.

Cory waited for the door to close and turned to her cousin. "Satin, tell Aunt Jane . . ."

"No. There is nothing for it. I must marry Sir Edward." Satin turned away. Cory touched her shoulder, and thus the girls stayed in silent contemplation for some moments. All Satin could think was: Oh, Nick, my own Wildfire, my dearest blue eyes . . . You were only a dream. You were never meant to be mine. I would have married someone in the end, it might as well be to someone who wants me so badly.

The drive to Brighton had been pleasant enough. Satin had exerted herself to entertain their crowded little group in her father's coach while her father played outrider on horseback. She was not going to break down. Over and over again she told herself that it would be fine, that all was well. She would think of Sir Edward's florid good looks and remind herself that at one time she had been very attracted to him. She would tell herself that the man she wanted would never be hers anyway. . . .

So she managed to smile and overflow with bubbling spirits, and Cory, only Cory, knew that Satin was nearly hysterical! They had not been installed in their Brighton lodgings for more than half a day when Maudly opened the parlor door and announced Sir Edward. Only Cory and Satin were there as Lady Jane and the earl had gone off in different directions. Cory eyed her cousin and decided to keep silent, but she was going to watch this exchange, and watch she did.

Sir Edward entered the room in his usual style. His curls were all in place, his cutaway of blue superfine fit his trim figure in high fashion, and Cory allowed him a certain charm, but she could see ruthlessness in his eyes. He went first to her and bent over her hand.

"Miss Bretton, what a delight you are to the sight. Yellow becomes you."

She inclined her head and said in the same social voice he had used, "Thank you, Sir Edward. Would you join us for tea? I can have Maudly bring in another cup."

"No, thank you. As a matter of fact"—he was already standing in front of Satin—"I was hoping to convince your cousin to come for a ride with me in my phaeton." He bent over her hand and his lips lingered on her wrist before he continued, "I know how much she enjoys a view of the sea." His voice was soft, and his eyes caressed as he turned to politely include Cory. "And perhaps you too would enjoy the ride?"

"No," said Miss Bretton just a bit more stiffly than she had intended. A cad, she thought. The man is a devil and a cad. He means to have Satin's heart as well as her hand, and he doesn't care how he goes about it, and Cory wasn't even sure that Sir Edward's heart was in it. He wasn't moved by love. By desire, perhaps, but not by love. "We only arrived this morning, and I think I will spend the day about the house getting settled in."

He turned to Satin. "My dear?" And then to indicate further that he was not about to take no for an answer from her, he added, "It will do you good to feel the salt air against your cheeks, and we may relax and continue our talk." This last was said on a low note.

"Yes," said Satin, thinking, might as well get it over with. "Thank you, I would enjoy that. I'll just take up my spencer and hat . . ." She looked to her cousin as she rose. "Are you certain you wouldn't like to join us, Cory?"

"No, I think not." It was hard for Cory to leave her cousin to her fate, but she felt that Satin was going to have to face this man and it might as well be now. They had to know if he could be dissuaded from his course and then they would have to act accordingly.

Satin sat quietly in the open phaeton for a while and allowed Sir Edward to chatter about the scenery and recent literary works in his droll and unalarming manner. Silently, she was thankful for his momentary sense of fair play. Perhaps he meant in earnest to win her love? No, her sixth sense warned her not to trust him, but at least at this moment she need not fear him. This, in turn, tickled her sense of the ridiculous and she could not help casting him a sideways glance and asking, "Well, if you are going to quote the Quarterly's review on poor Rodgers, then you must remember what they wrote about me!"

He looked at her in no little surprise before he burst into laughter. "By God, woman! You have a knack of catching a man unawares." And then, more seriously and to remind her of her position in society, he said, "The Quarterly did not realize they were reviewing a female's work when they looked kindly on *Passion's Seed*."

"No, they did not know the identity of the author, but they did write that it was 'an elegance, a wonderful love story that depicted our Prince Regent's set in all its glory.'" She eyed him again. "Indeed, they went so far as to say that it was wildly explicit and yet managed to miss being vulgar." She was satisfied that she had made her point.

"And, I repeat, they did not know it had been written by a woman, and our Prince Regent's set does not know it had been written by one of their own. One does not spy on one's friends and then ridicule them on paper," he returned on a hard note.

She bit her lip. "That is not what I did. Anyone could see that it was merely story telling with the age we live in as a backdrop. I wrote about people—as they are, for their enjoyment . . ."

"And for the entertainment of the middle classes. No. You wrote about our people, our own, for all to read and laugh about."

"No. If we cannot laugh at ourselves then we are not real," she threw back at him emotionally. "Those in our society who do not realize that have missed something in life."

"But they rule our way of life, those who do not see what you see, and they would put an end to your father's and your comfort in the world you must exist in," he answered, pulling in the phaeton, putting up the brake and turning to look down at her upturned face. How dark her eyes were. How they glistened with her emotions; how lovely she was.

"Sir Edward . . ." she started, her hand going to his chest in an entreaty.

He caught the gloved hand and held it to his heart. "Ned. I wish you to call me Ned, to feel close to me, to . . ."

"To what? To love you?" she returned desperately.

"Eventually," he answered.

What to do? She dove into her mind for an answer and came up with only a repartee. "And what shall I

do in answer to that? Shall I throw my arms round
your neck and tell you to kiss me and let the party
begin?"

He smiled. "You do know how to splash a man
with cold water, don't you?"

"Ask yourself why I wish to," she answered gravely.

"Satin, accept it. You shall be mine, and if you behave yourself, I would make an effort to make you
happy." He was taking her waist, drawing her to
him and bending to drop a kiss ever so lightly on her
pursed, cherry lips.

She did not resist. Here was the man she was
going to marry. She allowed him his kiss, dissecting
it in her mind. It was not, after all, repulsive, yet it
did nothing to her, nothing for her, and when he released her, she sighed.

"Sir Edward, is that what you want? For it is all I
have to give you." Her dark eyes touched him with
sadness.

He hardened. "Oh, no, my Satin, you have more,
much more lurking in you, and when the time comes
you will tremble to my touch."

"Tremble to your touch?" Her brow went up. "I
think not!"

He took a strong hold of her arm and held her
tightly pinned to his chest. "Satin, your blood races
through you, and don't ever doubt that I have the
ability to make it bubble. I will draw on your
emotions—"

"Indeed!" She cut him off. "But will it be love, sir,
or hate?"

They sat for a moment, eyeing one another, totally
unaware that they were being observed. The Duke of
Morland sat astride his fidgeting horse, the breakers
beating against the sand at his back, and if blood
ever raced and bubbled, it did so in his veins at that
precise moment. What was this? Why should he feel
thusly? he asked himself.

Satin and Sir Edward looked to be two lovers in the throes of a quarrel. He could almost see Satin's dark eyes flash. Yet something, he did not know what, just did not jibe. He had just come from Sir Frederick's lodgings. He had endured it all. Freddy's chatter about the ride into Brighton with Satin and Cory and the dry-witted Lady Jane. He had managed to inquire lightly if Satin seemed in "good spirits."

"Satin?" Sir Frederick had returned suddenly on a thoughtful note. "Odd that you should ask."

"Oh?" He had felt his heart beat at nearly double its rate. "Why?"

"Because I couldn't put my finger on it, Nick, but she didn't seem herself," Freddy had returned.

"Under the weather?" The duke tried not to appear too inquisitive.

"Could be . . . but I don't think that was it. Seemed faraway and not quite happy. In fact, asked Cory . . . Miss Bretton . . . about it."

"And?"

"Well, that's what confirmed it in my own head," Sir Frederick answered, nodding. "You see, Miss Bretton and I are, I hope, I believe, reaching an understanding and are therefore on . . . comfortable terms."

"I am pleased to hear it." The Duke smiled, touching his friend's shoulder. "You two are well suited, but what has that . . ."

"So, as you might imagine, Miss Bretton felt she could confide in me just a bit. She started to tell me that her cousin is suffering a devilishly tight situation, but we were then interrupted, you see, and she was unable to tell me the rest."

Unable to expand on this, the duke allowed the subject of Satin and her problem to be dropped from their conversation, but he came away from it feeling all the more troubled himself. Why he should feel anything at all was more than he could fathom. He had nought to do with Satin and whom she meant to marry. After all, Sir Edward was good ton, Sir Edward was . . .

Why could he not finish the thought? Because, you prime fool, you don't want any man to have her! He had finally answered the question. Damnation, he was in a muddle! What to do? Nought. Let it go. He looked at the two on the cliff's edge. Sir Edward had taken up the reins and was urging his pair on. If he didn't move out of range they would soon see him.

Indeed, why not cut the happy couple off and pay his respects? A wonderful notion. He spurred his horse forward and cantered up the sandy hill to the road so that he was soon riding abreast of the slow-moving phaeton. He tipped his hat and called out a jovial greeting.

Satin's mind reeled, and her heart warmed. Here was Wildfire. Oh, how she loved him. His blue eyes were beams of bright, soft heaven. She lost herself in those eyes as he spoke and scarcely heard what he said. Oh, Wildfire, if only you could save me, was her unconscious thought.

"And to Lady Satin," he said quietly, moving his horse closer to her side of the vehicle. He was bending over his knee, making a flourish of tipping his top hat. "May I extend my congratulations and wish you happy?"

She looked sharply from him to Sir Edward. So, Sir Edward had already instigated his plans. It angered her, all the more so because the duke seemed personally unaffected by the news.

"If that is what you wish to do," she answered, her dark eyes lowered.

"Satin, what is this?" He spoke only to her, his eyes caressed her. "You know whatever your decision for your future is, I would earnestly wish your happiness."

She brought her dark eyes up to his blue ones and they silently implored him. She did not dare say what was in her head. Not now, not here with Sir Edward at her side. How could she? She made the attempt, though, in spite of the obstacles around her.

"Nick, sometimes we appear to be what we are not. Sometimes we must do not what we want, but what we must, and those of us that can, make the best of it. Knowing that there is a friend somewhere nearby is a comfort . . . ." It was said in a hush of emotion, and she could read puzzlement on his face.

"This is all very touching," Sir Edward said on a dry note, "but I must see my lady home." He nodded curtly at the duke and whipped his horses off.

Wildfire sat his horse and watched as they drew away. Lady Satin did not turn around, but there was something in the droop of her delicate shoulders that was not like her. What had she meant? Was she being constrained to marry Sir Edward? Was that it? Was her father behind this? Was Sir Edward offering such a price that her father could not refuse? He knew that the earl was in financial difficulties . . .

Chapter Fifteen

The Prince Regent had brought Brighton into fashion when he elected to designate the resort spa as the location for his Royal Pavilion. This opulent, overdone, immense work of palatial magnificence was the center of the aristocracy's frenzy in Brighton. Around its borders everyone strutted, strolled, ogled, quizzed and buzzed.

The summer season had only just begun, but already the noble fashionables were about in force and bent on enjoying the best of all festivities in riotous frivolity. This aura of merrymaking was carried through the day when ladies of fashion meandered down the narrow stretch and tangle of streets known as The Lanes. Here they were sure to find the best of silks, china and tea. Brighton's regency squares, piers and promenades were full to overflowing during the long, sunny days; the nights in Brighton rivaled the days with their glittering routs and fêtes.

Lord Alvanly had the honor of hosting the first of Brighton's balls, and as he bent to his wife's satisfied sighs, he realized that the squeeze of people everywhere he looked was a sure sign of the affair's success.

The count had arrived in town early that morning and was quick to seek Satin out and to pull her onto the dance floor for a waltz. "Damn!" he breathed, then quickly apologized. "But just how can we dance with people bumping into us at every turn . . . ?"

Satin smiled absently as her mind was elsewhere.

He looked at her then. She was very lovely in her white muslin gown. Her dusky curls were in fine array round her piquant face, but something in her dark eyes caught his attention. "Satin?" He frowned. "What is it? What is wrong?"

"Wrong? Why, Otto, what could be wrong?"

"*You* tell me," he returned, for he knew her too well and there *was* something. He could feel it. Satin was not one who could easily hide away her feelings, though, in truth, most people would not have noticed her distress.

She looked at him for a long moment. Could she confide in Otto? No. He would rage and fume and rant, but he would not have the solution to her problem and in the end—in the end, all could be lost. "Nothing is wrong." She patted his large arm. "Really."

"You look pale," he answered in his way.

She laughed. "I do not. Now stop it, or you shall have me worried about my appearance."

Then they were interrupted on the dance floor and Sir Edward was smiling down at Satin. Otto pulled a face, but he had no choice and had to relinquish her hand. He looked at her to see if she would object, for then he would have danced away with her. She did not and he said quietly, "I will see you later, Satin." There was a meaning in his eyes.

"The good count watches over you," said Sir Edward.

"With gentlemen as yourself lurking about, 'tis no wonder," she returned testily and surprised herself.

"Oooh. The lady's tongue is sharp tonight." He smiled at her, not in the least perturbed by her open dislike.

"Do you find the truth so?" she countered, her eyes doing battle with him.

"Satin," he said gravely, "the truth is that you will be mine, so accept it." He was holding her in his firm grasp as he waltzed her round the floor. With these words his white-gloved hand tightened round hers, and his other hand brought her waist closer to him still. "In the end, you will find yourself in my arms."

She blanched. The effrontery of the man. How dare he take such hold of her in public! She wanted to slap his face. No, she must not create a scene. Ignore his hold. She went to war. "Accept it? You mistake your power, sir. You would have to find yourself a mighty philter, for it will take nothing less for me to accept it."

His grip dug into her flesh, for she was irritating his sense of self, wounding his ego. "For now the only love potion I need, my dear, is the truth I hold over you."

"A ball and chain is not a love potion." She felt herself trembling beneath his hold. How could she marry him? How would she go on? How could she endure his touch?

Anyone intimate with Satin watching her in that moment would have realized in an instant that she was undergoing some emotional strain. Therefore, it was not surprising that Cory cut off her conversation with Sir Frederick to watch her cousin thoughtfully. "Freddy," she said after a moment's hesitation, "I wish you were able to dance."

"Would love to accommodate you, my dear, broken arm n'all," he offered devotedly, bowing gallantly.

She smiled. "No, no, I mean to save Satin . . ."

"Why?" asked a strong, male voice at her back. "Is Lady Satin in need of saving?"

She looked round and saw the duke, tall and grim, stepping purposely forward. He did not bother to smile a greeting, which was something of an indication of his mood the last few days.

Cory attempted a light rejoinder. "I was just remarking that my cousin looks a bit . . . fatigued."

"Were you?" He looked thoughtfully at Satin. "I don't agree. She looks"—he hesitated—"spirited, rather flushed, but certainly not fatigued." Something was afoot. What it was he could not yet guess, but get to its heart he suddenly decided he must do.

"Indeed," Sir Frederick put in, looking from his friend to Miss Bretton. Obviously, Cory was distressed over Satin and Sir Edward. "I think Lady Satin needs a bit of fresh air." He smiled sweetly at his love. "Shall I take her off, my dear?"

"No need," the duke put in at once. "You attend Miss Bretton, Freddy. I'll see to Satin."

Cory put a gloved hand on his lower arm, detaining him momentarily. "Your grace, it may not be so easy . . . to rescue her from herself."

"Nothing, Miss Bretton, will ever be easy with Lady Satin, yet I rather think I may contrive," he returned with a rueful smile.

Cory watched him make his way through the throng of dancers on the floor. He was certainly the man Satin needed. She could see that. He had the experience, the self-assurance and the skill to handle all that life offered. Would that he could rescue Satin from herself—from Sir Edward!

Sir Edward felt his shoulder being tapped. It was nearly the end of the waltz, so he managed a friendly enough smile as he turned. The smile froze on his face as he saw who it was interrupting his dance with Satin.

"Nick," he said on a hard note, "a bit late, aren't you?"

"No, I don't think so. I rather think I am just in the nick of time." Then jovially enough, "Here, now give over gracefully. You will have her all to yourself soon enough, Ned."

Sir Edward had no choice. He couldn't very well create a scene on the ballroom floor without appearing a fool. He inclined his head and moved gracefully out of their way. The duke lost no time. Quickly, he steered Satin out of Sir Edward's view. Before she could question, object, he had her slender arm and was at the ballroom door pulling her out into the courtyard and the warm night air.

Outdoors the sky above was a blue black velvet touched with a sprinkling of glittering stars. The moon was a crescent hanging on its own and appearing to grin at its companions. The breeze was full with early summer's sweet scents and laced with the salt from the sea air. Satin looked at Wildfire with a sudden aching yearning. All she wanted at that moment was to collapse into his arms. All she wanted was to go into his embrace. All she wanted was to whisper his name. So, without further ado, she gave over to those needs and breathing his name huskily she found his touch.

Here she was, this woman-child with the large dark eyes and the full cherry lips. Here she was, looking up at him with an expression that filled him with desire and emotion. He reached for her, and she went to him willingly. He heard his name on her lips and he bent to hold her closer as his mouth sought hers. His kiss was long, tender and blossoming into another when he attempted to recall where they were. She wouldn't allow it. When he would have put her away, she held on to him tightly and encouraged yet another kiss from his lips as hers parted, and she pressed her body against his hardness.

He did set her away then, and she murmured his name. "Nick, oh, Nick, don't you want me?"

"Satin, ah, babe, of course I want you, but not like this—not when you are in trouble and desperate and you don't know where to turn."

She frowned and her eyes lowered beneath his penetrating glance. "I . . . I didn't say I was in trouble . . ."

"You didn't have to," he returned and took her chin in his gloved fingers. "Satin, why are you marrying Sir Edward?"

She looked at him then and in a voice that was breaking said, "I have to . . ."

"You have to?" he nearly shouted. "Why in thunder do you have to? Is it money? Does your father need the money from the marriage settlement?"

She shook her head. "No, it isn't the money . . . now."

"Satin, if it is, you have only to tell me and I would make arrangements for your father to have it."

She looked at him. "So that you could buy me for a mistress?" she smiled softly. "That isn't done. One doesn't buy a mistress—a virgin mistress from his own class."

"Satin," he said softly, gently, "I am not ready to get married, but I want you and I would protect you and your reputation. No one need ever know."

She was not insulted. She knew him too well, but her answer was firm. Even if she were not being forced to marry Sir Edward, she could not accept such an arrangement, not even from Wildfire, who she adored with all her heart and soul. "But Nick, *I* would know."

He took her shoulders and brought her to him, and this time his kiss was nearly fierce with the onslaught of his passion. She responded, but to her the kiss was good-bye. She heard him breathe in her ear, "This—this is insane, isn't it?"

She knew he was referring to the fact that whatever happened, no matter how much time elapsed, they seemed to find themselves in one another's arms, wanting one another and yet so far apart still. "Yes, yes, it is . . ." And then because there was more she wanted to say and couldn't, "Oh, Nick."

"Very touching." Sir Edward's hard, dry tones split the fantasy of their privacy and shattered their dreams.

Wildfire stepped in front of Satin to confront Sir Edward. "Do you think so, sir?" he responded easily. "Indeed, I must agree with you."

Sir Edward moved forward ominously to meet

Wildfire's glittering blue eyes. *"I could bury you for this!"*

The duke's smile was dangerous. "I am most willing to allow you to try."

Satin touched Wildfire's arm. "Nick?" Her voice was scarcely a whisper. If they were not careful they would attract undue attention and create a scandal.

He patted her gloved hand reassuringly. "I am certain, however," he said to Sir Edward, "that we may give one another satisfaction in this matter at another, more appropriate time."

"You are right, of course." Sir Edward was already calming himself. He bent his arm to Satin. "My lady, you will come with me?" It was not really a question.

Satin cast the duke one quick glance that begged him not to interfere as she placed her hand on Sir Edward's arm and allowed him to lead her away.

The duke stood and watched them reenter the ballroom. This was more than he could bear! What hold did Ned have over Satin? Why would she go away with him so meekly? What was it? What could he do? What would he do? And damn it all to blazes, he had to do something!

Chapter Sixteen

Affairs had progressed quite comfortably for Miss
Bretton and Sir Frederick. It was noted amongst his
friends that "dear Freddy" was looking his old self
again, that he seemed happier than he had been in
two years and that it was very nearly certain he was
in love with the "Bretton chit."

So it was that a summer afternoon two days after
the Alvanly ball found Miss Bretton beneath her
parasol enjoying a ride in Sir Frederick's open curricle. There was no tiger in attendance and, as his
broken arm made his handling of the reins more
than just a bit difficult, he was pleased enough to
give the reins over to Miss Bretton and to discover
yet another one of her many capabilities.

"It appears that I am in love with a notable whip!"
he announced after she wielded the curricle through
Brighton's traffic and negotiated a tricky turn onto
the dockside avenue.

She looked at him sharply, and he reprimanded
her, saying severely, "Careful now, or I shall have to
take that back. You nearly ran that poor old woman
down."

"Take what back?" she managed to say without
looking at him. "That I am an accomplished whip
—or that you are in love with me?" She felt herself
blush. He had not mentioned love; he had not tried to
kiss her since that day back at the inn, and she had
been in a bout of confusion and doubt over the prob-

lem. Oh, he had certainly been friendly and atten-
tive. He had been gallant and flirtatious, but he had
not been serious and he had not mentioned love
again until this moment.

He was quiet for a space of time, then he took the
reins from her with his good hand and pulled his
team to a stop along the sandy edge of the road. The
breakers were softly rolling, picking up pebbles and
throwing them back, and the sound was oddly sooth-
ing in the background.

"Cory," he said, and when she did not look at him,
for suddenly she was hurt and her pride terribly
pinched, "Cory, look at me."

She turned, and her hazel eyes rose to meet his
blue ones. "Yes?"

"I tried to tell you about my past—and you
wouldn't hear it. I find that I cannot—will not—
pursue you in earnest until you know all there is to
know about me."

"I see," she answered. Then she surprised herself
by adding, "Then perhaps you should take me home,
for I have been under the false impression that you
were pursuing me . . . are still . . ."

"Cory," he said on an exasperated note, "you
know what I am talking about. Why are you making
it difficult for me?"

"Because you have puffed up this past of yours until it weighs more than reality. I don't care about the
past. If you tell me you were a murderer, I will say:
'Oh, were you? You must not be anymore.'" She
took his hand and held it to her cheek. "Can't you
see that all you are now is what I want?"

He had blanched when she had given him the
analogy. He withdrew his hand. "But, Cory, there
were some who said *I* was a murderer!"

She opened her hazel eyes wide. "I see you are determined to shock me. Well, then, have at me."

He released a long-drawn breath. "I was involved

with a young woman two and a half years ago . . .
she was a tradesman's daughter. She—she became
pregnant with my child and wanted me to marry
her." He looked imploringly at Cory. "I was not in
love with her, Cory. I suppose I behaved the cad. I offered to take care of her and the child always. She
was distraught, she was beside me in my curricle at
the time and she became violently upset. She began
to strike at me while I was handling my team
through London traffic. I—I still don't know exactly
what happened. I warded off a blow just as the horses
reared off some vehicle they had nearly run into. She
went off the side and was hit by yet another oncom-
ing vehicle. She was killed."

"My poor Freddy," was Miss Bretton's reaction as
she put her hand to his cheek. "It wasn't your
fault."

"There was an inquest and they, too, found me
nonculpable, yet there were whispers. You see the
circumstances involved made it all look suspicious."

She said nothing for a time, and then she spoke
softly. "And so hidden away it will lurk above your
head and forever haunt you."

"And the woman whom I take for wife . . ." he said
gravely.

She touched his cheek again. "Oh, Freddy, it
wouldn't haunt me. I would not be outraged at the
whispers, and there will always be people who will
point and whisper. I won't be ashamed." Her eyes
held him with the strength of her affection. "I
know what I know and those who matter to us will
know the same, that you are innocent of murder."
She sighed. "As to the other thing, about your
being the father of her child, I hope I am worldly
enough to understand that such things happen
and that she was probably as much to blame as
yourself."

He took her hand from his cheek and kissed it fervently. "Cory, my love, I wish I had found you sooner. . . ."

"There." She laughed. "We have settled your past and now there is only the future. But, Freddy, I am terribly worried about Satin, and this time I don't see a way out."

"You are speaking of Sir Edward's suit?" he returned, his light brows drawing into a frown. "I don't think I really understand why Satin feels compelled to marry him."

"Compelled? Freddy, she is being blackmailed into this marriage!"

"Blackmailed?" He was shocked. "Good God! Cory, what can you mean?"

"Oh, I can't tell you . . ." She looked away. What was she going to do?

Sir Charles patted his horse's neck and eased him away from the park's traffic. He looked at the duke with some concern. "Nick? I say, Nick, are you attending me?"

"What? Yes, of course. You think we should leave immediately. Right now, without a word to anyone, and make our way unnoticed back to London to scotch an assassination plot against the Prince Regent."

Sir Charles opened his eyes wide. "Well, I must say you are taking the news famously. I tell you that a plot to kill our Prince Regent is underway, and you behave as though it is the merest commonplace."

"Do I? That is because I believe the information you have received to be without foundation."

"Oh, really?" Sir Charles took affront. "And when have you known me to be an alarmist?"

The duke gazed at his cousin and frowned. "That is the perplexing thing. Never. In fact, had this piece of news come from anyone else I would have laughed it off. Coming from you, I am attempting to make sense of it."

"Nick, I agree with you. It does not seem likely that the frogs have instituted a plan to assassinate Prinny just now; however, my source says they will do anything to prevent the third coalition from going into effect."

"Yes, but the prince is here in Brighton," objected the duke.

"Wrong." Sir Charles could not prevent the smug look from taking command of his pleasant features. "He left Brighton this very morning for London. An emergency meeting was called in secret at the Home Office which required his presence. He has, in fact, traveled back to London incognito."

The duke's blue eyes glittered with amusement. "Never say so! Damn, but that is entertaining. Tell me, who gave him the notion to disguise himself?"

Charles coughed into his gloved hand. "Something he read . . ."

They exchanged glances and burst out laughing, but the duke pursued the matter. "Come on, Chuck, if it wasn't you who trussed him up, then who?"

"Oh, as to that, I may have put him on to the notion, but the rest was all his doing, I assure you, though I did object when he wanted to dress up as a Spanish count."

"What did he go as?"

Charles looked at the duke for a long moment. "A, hmmm, groom."

This did, in fact, totally amaze the duke and he said so. "Damn! Are you telling me that Prinny accepted mussing up his hair and dirtying his face?"

"And don a groom's best Sunday clothes as well, and they, my Nicky, were such that one had to stand out of the room to bear up to the stench. Then off he went on some miserable cob with security following at a discreet distance. By now I believe the newness of the lark is wearing off, and by the time he reaches London I expect he will be in very bad humor."

"Charles, old boy, you astound me!" The duke laughed. "But before I rush off to London with you, satisfy me on one point."

"What then?"

"Sidmouth, what does he say to all this?"

"Nick, really!" Sir Charles returned on a surprised note. "Where is your mind? Do you think for one moment that I would have come to you if Sidmouth and the Home Office were not behind me?"

Lord Wildfire sighed. There didn't seem to be a way out of this. He was going to have to leave Brighton and Lady Satin. It tore him apart. Satin. She loomed in his mind and he knew how much he wanted her. He was willing to surrender to his passion for her now, and he had to tell her that he wanted her to be his wife! There, once again he allowed the words to enter his head. His wife . . . Satin.

There was Sir Edward putting a rub in his way and causing Satin some torment. Why? How to deal with it? He had to save Satin from herself. He had to get Satin to confide in him, and how would he do this if he were in London? He eyed his cousin. "Charles, there is someone I must see before we go. . . ."

"Satin?" It was more a statement than a question. If it had only just dawned on the duke recently that he was falling in love with the madcap Satin, his cousin had been much quicker to surmise the situation.

The duke shot him a look. "Have I been that transparent?"

Sir Charles smiled. "I know you, my Nick, and

more than that, I know Satin. You two were inevitable and lord help you both."

The duke grinned. "Do I take that for approval or warning?"

"Both." Sir Charles smiled. "And yes, approval. If I couldn't have the lady to wife myself, I might as well have her as a cousin."

"Well, you shan't have her for either if we don't conclude our business in London quickly."

"Why?" Sir Charles frowned. "What do you mean?"

"The lady in question has been persuaded to accept Sir Edward's suit," said the duke grimly.

"What?" It was a shriek. "Impossible. Satin would never marry Ned!"

"That is what I thought, but I had the news from Ned himself."

"Confirmed by Satin?"

"In a way," the duke answered thoughtfully. "That is why I have to see her before we leave."

"Not wise. You will end in telling her you don't go to London for another woman. I know Satin, she will wheedle the truth out of you, and we are not in a position to give her the truth."

"But . . ." the duke started to object.

Sir Charles gazed at him in some amazement. Here was Wildfire, rakehell of hearts, pining to answer to a woman, a chit of a woman! It was incredible. "Nick, you know better," was what he managed to say.

"So I do." Lord Wildfire sighed. "And still I will jot her off a note of sorts. Chuck, this situation with Ned worries me."

"Well, and so it might, but he can't whisk her off to the altar in the few days we are off to London after all," answered Sir Charles reasonably.

"No, but he can send in the announcement . . ." Then the duke knew what he would write in that note. "Unless I can get my Satin to stall him—and perhaps I can." With a sudden decision he whirled his horse around. "Come on, Chuck, we have no time to lose!"

Chapter Seventeen

Sir Edward Danton considered himself a knowing individual with a certain sixth sense. He was not wrong in his self-analysis. He eyed the lady he had chosen to marry and knew that her mind was working to find a way out of her predicament. She was stalling for time, she was looking for an answer and as of yet had not found one; however, he did not trust her in this. She was too capable a little devil and just might find a way around his threat. He couldn't risk it. What to do? The answer came slowly, wrapping itself around his mind, and when it settled he smiled to himself.

Satin looked askance at him. She didn't like that smile and so stated warily, "What is it, Ned? Why are you grinning like that? You look positively wicked!"

"Do I? I was thinking of you," he answered softly.

She reached out across the sofa from her corner and touched his arm. "Ned, please, won't you stop thinking of me? Can't you see we just won't suit? I—I don't love you." She attempted to placate him. "Oh, you are wondrously handsome, a very fine figure of a man, and no doubt you have a certain attraction, but to force a woman, such as myself, to marry you can only put us at opposite ends. Don't you see?"

"What I see, Satin, is you in my bed . . . is you bearing my name, my children, and, in time, happy to do so," he answered, reaching out to touch her cheek.

She pulled away from his hand and grimaced. "You are a scoundrel."

"Of necessity," he answered. "As we are, all of us, when the need arises."

"No, I would not do to you as you do to me—in spite of your cruelty."

"Satin," he said softly and drew her to him on the sofa. She pulled away hard and he fought to hold her in place. "Think about how much happier you will be when you have accepted the inevitable." He stood up abruptly. There were things he was going to do and they had to be done at once. He gave her a quick, polite inclination of the head. "I will see you tonight for dinner."

"As you wish." At least her aunt had invited enough people for dinner. She would do what she could to avoid being alone with him. Oh, Nick, where are you? She hadn't seen him all day. She had taken a morning ride with Otto in the park hoping to see Wildfire there, but she hadn't, and her mood was now quite despondent. She watched Sir Edward leave. What was she going to do?

Candlelight glowed, there was the soft fragrance of summer floating through the open window of the dining room. There was the gentle mumur of voices in light dinner conversation over a well-dressed Waverly dinner table, and Lady Jane Bretton looked around at her guests with some satisfaction until her aged eyes rested on Sir Edward.

A frown descended over her features, and she touched and played with her long diamond earring as she considered him. He was gazing at Satin possessively and he had such a purposeful expression that she felt a shiver go up her spine.

She knew, of course, that Satin had accepted to marry the man. Waverly knew it, too, and though there was nothing to object to in the match, they both were uneasy about it. Satin, poor child, seemed distraught over it, yet she would insist on it when they attempted to reason with her.

Otto leaned into his chair and laughed. "Tell you what, Satin, Prinny was only just saying the other night that this author, the one that wrote that outrageous new novel, had made himself immortal. Said he preferred it over every other Gothic he has ever read and means to discover where the author hides himself."

"Really?" Satin managed to breathe. "I have always preferred the works of a man like Walter Scott and his *The Lay of the Last Minstrel* to any piece of romantic nonsense such as *Passion's Seed.*"

"Yes," agreed Sir Edward at once, "though, in truth, Scott's *Marmion* has always held a special fascination for me. The notion of a knight riding hard to take up his intended bride and escape with her under the noses of all her family is most . . . exciting."

Satin felt a strange chill. "I have enjoyed *Marmion* as well, for its poetry and pace as well as its plot." She turned to Otto. "You, I think, would prefer *The Lady of the Lake.*"

Otto waved this off and took another helping of potatoes.

"No, like Ned, I am for the knight in *Marmion.* How dare they try to marry his woman off to some fop while he is off fighting. I love the way Scott handles that piece."

Sir Edward smiled, for he could see Satin fidget until her cousin changed the subject. "Tyson," Cory stuck in gently, "has been training his beagles, you know. When Sir Frederick and I were out this morning we came upon him. They seem to be coming along nicely."

"Bah!" the count returned. "Beagles! What is it next to fox hunting? What could compare to fox hunting?"

"Stag hunting," answered Sir Edward.

"That is quite dreadful," said Satin. "I have always been repulsed by it."

"Absurd child," returned Sir Edward, "a hunt is a hunt. What makes fox hunting acceptable over the hunting of deer?"

"A fox is a cunning killer. A deer is nature's gift to the forest," she said quietly. "There is a world of difference. A fox will kill a farmer's chickens for the pleasure of the kill and not even bother to eat what he has destroyed."

Otto nodded. "Answer that, Ned!"

"The deer destroys the farmer's crops," was his answer.

"Enough!" said Lady Jane. "This is not fit conversation for the table. Kill . . . destroy . . . stop it." She turned to her brother and introduced a new topic. "I have heard that the Stael is due to arrive shortly. Is it true, do you think?"

Satin's mind wandered off. The conversation retreated into the background as did the company and the untouched food before her. That afternoon she had received a note from the duke and she had read and reread it so many times that the words stood out in her mind's eye even now.

Dearest Satin,

Sir Charles drags me to London though it is my inclination to remain here with you just now.

My love, trust me and don't do anything foolish. Only wait for my return.

Nick

It was short and it was certainly sweet, but what did it mean? Trust him? Don't do anything foolish? Wait for his return? Well, she would certainly try, if he would only hurry. She sighed. What could he do? Even if he wanted to help her, how could he? Ned meant to expose her if she did not marry him. She would stall the announcement, but sooner or later he would take control. Faith! She was in such a bind.

"What are you dreaming about?" It was Sir Edward who held the position on her right. Otto was on her left and chuckling over the latest *on-dit*. She attempted to smile and look interested.

"I said," Sir Edward was not to be put off, "what are you dreaming about?"

She looked at him. "My dreams are my own."

He stiffened. "Why do you fight me?"

"Because you created the setting and, sir, it is a battlefield."

"No, Satin, if only you would see."

Her aunt came to the rescue by suggesting that they leave the gentlemen to their port and their cigars while the ladies withdrew to the parlor. Satin was quick to stand up and take Cory's hand for she felt herself shaking. How much more of this could she bear?

Cory shot her a penetrating look and said under her breath, "Calm yourself. Come, we'll talk. . . ."

"Talking won't help any longer," Satin answered on a hard note. "I might as well just give in and admit I am beaten."

"Since when do you give up so easily? No, my dear, you are not so poor-spirited."

"Cory, he means to ruin the name of Waverly if I don't marry him, and I have come to understand the man. He would carry out his threat—he would." It was almost a wail.

"We'll find a way—we must, if only you can keep him from sending in an announcement."

"I have done that. I have told him that I would refute any announcement that went in before next week as I need the time to get used to the idea of our marriage." She frowned. "He doesn't quite believe me, but he has agreed to allow me the time."

"Well, then, by next week we must come up with a solution to the problem," answered Cory, "somehow."

* * *

Hyde Park stretched out in rolling undulations of green turf, sparkling fountains and summer flowers. Nannies walked with their charges in tow. Dogs romped and played with their masters and created a peaceful scene. Indeed, as most of London had moved on to summer resorts for the season, the park was practically devoid of its usual strutting fashionables.

Two gentlemen, however, stood out among the pedestrians. Both nobility. Both well-dressed Corinthians, one taller and unmistakably far more rakish than the other, but both following at a discreet distance the movements of a brightly clad young female.

"What Molly Jenkins has to do with Marmont is more than I can fathom," said Sir Charles on a grumbling note.

"Chuck, you surprise me," returned the duke, one brow up quizzically.

"No, what I mean is what she has to do with all this business."

"Again, you astound me." The duke was grinning.

Sir Charles took umbrage. "I am no noddy, but I fail to see what we can possibly discover by following the pretty piece about."

"Ah," said the duke, but he was commenting meaningfully on the fact that the lady in question had stopped to converse with an individual the duke recognized all too well. "So, Miss Jenkins is acquainted with old Savant!"

Sir Charles's mouth dropped, and he stood still beside his cousin as they watched Miss Jenkins pass something into the hands of the elderly Frenchman. "I can't believe it," breathed Charles. "What has Savant to do with all this?"

"He is against the third coalition," said the duke grimly. "And still I find it hard to believe that he would stoop to assassination . . ."

"What is to be done now?" Sir Charles was pulling at his lower lip.

"I suggest one of us furthers his acquaintance with Miss Jenkins," said the duke thoughtfully.

"I have never been in the petticoat line . . . You would be better at the game, Nick."

The duke sighed. "Perhaps, but my heart, Chuck, my heart won't be in it."

"No? Well, perhaps you may yet enjoy yourself, anyway!" said his cousin dryly.

The duke laughed. "Famous! I have made you a cynic at last."

While the duke and Sir Charles were steeped in political intrigue, Sir Edward was absorbed with his machinations to have Satin. There was a moment when he paused and it occurred to him that he was *too* intent on having her. He told himself that something was lacking, perhaps the right emotion, for he could not admit to any tenderness of feeling; yet even so, having begun on this road, he meant to see it through.

Off he went to Hove and applied for a special license. Satin was of age and he anticipated no problem here and incurred none. This done he found himself, in the same town, a minister of nondescript ethics and prepaid the man for his services. He then went to the circulating library and took up a book on potions and drugs for there was a possibility that Satin might have to be tranquilized throughout these planned proceedings.

There left only one last step to complete. He had to get hold of Satin and have her away for some hours before their movements would be detected and perhaps traced. This was proving to be the most difficult of all the tasks he had undertaken. For one thing, Cory had set herself up as a guardian of Satin. The two seemed to go everywhere in each other's company. In the last two days he had been unable even

to see Satin alone in the quiet of her parlor. Cory forever hovered in the merriest of moods and with a de-
termination to protect.

Right, then, one must first dispose of the wise Miss
Bretton before one could get at Lady Satin. He
thought of this for some length of time before a slow,
wicked smile spread across his handsome face. Indeed, he rather thought he just might have the solution to this, his last obstacle!

Chapter Eighteen

It was a gray summer morning of mist and fog. Sir Frederick winced as he squeezed into his pale yellow waistcoat and then again when he pulled on his light blue superfine cutaway coat after that. He turned to the long, gilt-edged mirror and frowned, for he did not like the final effect of this combination. He was not, however, about to trouble himself to change and decided that his Cory would be pleased enough; if she wasn't, he would allow her to take charge of such matters when they were neatly married. This thought brought a smile to his lips.

A knock sounded and a moment later his valet appeared with a silver tray extended. This proved to hold an ivory envelope of no particular style, and with a curious expression he dismissed his man and proceeded to break open the seal. He unfolded a note and read:

> Dearest Frederick,
>   Something dreadful has happened and there isn't any time to explain. We need you. Please meet us at the Lewes Inn, just outside Lewes by noon today and say nothing about where you are going to anyone who might tell my uncle or aunt.
>
>   Corine

What? Both of Sir Frederick's brows were up. Just what did this mean? What had happened? This wasn't like Cory. He reread the scrawled sentences again. Women! Strange beings forever talking in mysteries and riddles. Well, there was nothing for it. He would send for his carriage and make his way north to Lewes! Why Lewes?

Of all the outlandish places to meet! But, then, no doubt the inn was some charming little place the girls had fallen in love with. Women! Strange creatures, indeed, but made to be pampered. So it was that without further ado Sir Frederick made ready to leave for Lewes.

As he was doing so, his love was also opening an envelope, but hers was marked confidential. It brought a deepening frown to her face as she read:

Dearest Corine:
   As it happens I have discovered that Sir Edward plans to have your cousin, Lady Satin, one way or another. We must handle this carefully and without distressing her any further on the subject.
   She has agreed to meet him at the Lewes Inn, where they will be married in secret. Perhaps if we are there to stop the scoundrel, your cousin may yet be spared. Do not try and talk her out of this, as they will only change their plans. Simply go to the Brighton Hostlery where I have hired a post chaise to take you and your maid to Lewes. Don't worry, we shall stop this! Tell no one.
                              Your servant always,
                              Frederick

When Sir Edward had penned this note, he had been wise enough to muse at length over it and to choose his words carefully. All he knew of Miss Cory Bretton told him that she would not be easily fooled. Thus he had put together just enough to cause her doubt, just enough to make her worry and just enough to make her see that she must not attempt to discuss the letter with Satin.

He had been fairly certain that Cory's presence during the last few days meant that Satin had confided everything to her. Right, then, Cory knew that Satin was being blackmailed into this marriage. Cory knew that Satin was sacrificing her life to spare her father shame. It was a gamble, but an educated one that Miss Bretton would do as her Frederick wished and go to Lewes. So Miss Bretton and Sir Frederick would be to the north and out of the way while Satin . . . ah, Satin! . . . she would be rushing off to the southwest. How perfectly satisfying at last!

He was not far off. Miss Bretton sat with this note for some time. She was undecided. She was *not* impulsive. She was not an alarmist. She would not run off willy-nilly wherever she was told simply because she had been told (even by someone she loved) that it was the correct thing to do. What did Freddy mean by "take your maid"? She did not have one and he knew it. How odd. Perhaps he meant for her to take Maudly? It was impossible to do so without alerting Lady Jane to the fact that she was off . . .

What to do? She sighed over the question, troubled over the question and inquired of Maudly where Lady Satin was. She was told that Satin had gone to the stables to take out her horse for a ride on the beach. Deuce take the girl, thought Cory. Without a word to anyone? Then she sucked in breath. Could it be that Satin was already off for Lewes? Would Satin ride on horseback to Lewes? Faith and certes! Cory was on her feet and taking up her spencer and bonnet as she called out to Maudly that she was just going out for a spell to visit with a nearby friend, and, before anyone could object, she was out of the house.

* * *

This left only Satin, and she was not riding on the beach by anything but design, and the design was not of her making. She, too, had received a note that morning, but unlike Sir Frederick's and Cory's, this one made no secret of its author. It came from Sir Edward and was hard, cool and unbending:

Dearest heart,
   Don't doubt that you are that, or will be when you begin to respond to my courtship. Ride alone on Westly Beach where I shall meet you. Tell no one that you mean to do so, tell no one that you are meeting me, and perhaps I may discuss with you a revision of my plan to marry you. Perhaps I will give you more time if you are kinder to me. Meet me and we shall see.
         Your very obedient and adoring servant,
         Ned

Satin had read this and had doubted every word. She couldn't refuse the request, but she was certainly suspicious of it. Hence, she left a message with Maudly that she was off for a ride on the beach and that she should be back within a reasonable length of time. This done, and with some misgiving in her heart, she donned her green riding habit with its matching top hat and took up her gloves. It didn't take her long to have her horse tacked up and not much longer after that to make her way to the beach road.

Sir Edward Danton took stock of himself in the long, oak-framed looking glass of his bedroom. His auburn curls were fashioned in the popular style known as *à la Brutus* and it complemented his lean, good-looking countenance. His features, he conceded to himself, were not quite perfectly comely, but all in all he rather liked the total picture. His eyes, he noted, were sharp, bright and rich hazel beneath his well-defined dark brows. His lips were thin and firm, and his jaw was most certainly masculine. Indeed, everything was there for a woman to admire. Why then did Satin not?

He frowned and appraised his figure. He was noted for his fashion and could find nothing to fault in the cut of his buckskin riding coat and the tight-fitting buff breeches. His Hessians were topped with the sign of the fox hunter and were wonderfully polished. His figure was lean, yet manly enough, and his height (perhaps he was not as tall as the duke) was certainly nothing to sneer at. Why then did Satin sneer? She behaved as though he were some monster, as though his presence repulsed her. Why? It had not always been thus. In fact, he could remember still her dark eyes lighting up with laughter and warm invitation. . . .

Perhaps it was because he was forcing her hand? Indeed, she was a contrary chit and no doubt her irritation of nerves stemmed from that fact. No doubt. What then to do? Proceed. In the end she would come to accept and enjoy her situation. In time she would warm to his hand and even look for his kisses. In time.

Damn! Enough of these musings. He would school the chit and teach her to please him. After all, she was only a female. Once she was his, everything would fall into place. He took up his riding gloves, his top hat and his crop and made his way across the room. He had hired a coach for this expedition as it wouldn't do to be seen with Satin in his own carriage with his crest emblazoned upon the doors. Eyebrows would go up, and he didn't want to attract any undue interest until he was well away from Brighton. . . .

The duke looked his cousin over and grimaced. "Well, and when I tell you next time that you and the Home Office are out, perhaps you will believe me!"

"Don't be so smug! We couldn't very well ignore a threat on Prinny's life, now could we?"

"Of course not, but then it did not really require 'all the King's horses and all the King's men' to discover the threat was no more than a hoax," returned the duke in less than good humor.

Sir Charles eyed him. "Under ordinary circumstances you would not be so put out over this business."

"No? Then perhaps you will admit that these are not ordinary circumstances."

"Aren't they? In what way? You took out some time from your frivolous pursuits to indulge in your natural inclination for espionage and intrigue. It's right in your line to do so. What then has you so irritated?"

The duke frowned. "Satin. I just did not want to leave her when we did."

"Why?"

"It is not anything I can explain. My inclination for intrigue, perhaps?" the duke returned on a lighter note.

"Tell me, Nick, what do you mean by her?" Sir Charles was serious now.

"What do I mean by her? An interesting question and one I have yet to answer." He sighed. "Damn if I know!"

"Famous! You are itching to return to Brighton to look at Lady Satin and you don't know why? Stuff and nonsense!"

"You are being very polite when I can feel you burning to tell me off," the duke returned quizzically.

"Yes, and so I am. Do you mean to have her? Answer me that!"

"Charles, tread easy. What I mean to do is to return to Brighton and ascertain for myself if she means to have Sir Edward because she wants him. That is what I mean to do—for now."

"You know that she doesn't want him."

"Do I? Away from her now, I don't know anything of the sort. Women are very good at playacting for their own reasons."

"Nick! We are speaking of Satin. She is guileless, not quite the innocent to be sure, but she is not playing a game in this."

"Then why the secret engagement? What is it about Ned that has her tied to him?"

"That is another thing," returned Sir Charles. "Are you sure that is the case?"

"I told you, I had it from Ned himself," the duke riposted impatiently. "And very nearly confirmed by Satin as well."

Sir Charles shook his head. "I find it hard to believe."

"Then let us make haste and find out from the lady herself," answered the duke.

Chapter Nineteen

The sky was overcast and every few moments a cloud would shed some of its precipitation. There was a cool sea breeze and together with the mist created a damp that sent a shiver through Satin as she schooled her horse down the beach road. The sound of carriage wheels grinding against pebbles and sand made her look over her shoulder. She frowned. Could this be Sir Edward? It was not his traveling coach and those were not his carriage horses.

The driver of the cumbersome vehicle called out a halt and put on his brake as he brought his horses to a stop, and Satin's fine brows went up in surprise. It was Sir Edward. Well, why was he in a hired conveyance? Something like a warning began ringing in the back of her mind. Stupid girl, she told herself, don't allow your wild imagination to take hold. There is a reason for this.

Sir Edward hopped out easily and a few hard strides brought him to her. He smiled. "How lovely you look in the morning mist, my dear." It was an easy greeting full of his ready charm.

Right. An easy greeting that did not put her at her ease at all. Something was wrong, but what? She attempted to be herself and smiled in return. "You are also looking very well, sir."

He put his gloved hands on her waist and helped her down from her sidesaddle. His voice was gentle enough as he was careful not to frighten her. "Come then, Satin, it is time we talked."

There was nothing in that to send her into convulsions, was there? But she wanted to run. Ridiculous girl, she told herself. Run? Run from what? Run from whom, Sir Edward? Why? What could he do? There was a driver in attendance and the heart of the city at their backs.

Yet something in her mind cried: Run, Satin, run. Something in her heart called: Danger, danger, danger!

"Where is your coach, sir?" She eyed him before allowing him to lead her forward, though he had already tethered her horse at the rear of the coach.

"One of the axles was bent and it is in for repair. I found it easier just to hire a coach for the morning," he answered glibly.

There, she told herself, a reasonable answer. Right? Of course, reasonable. Run, Satin, run, the voice said again. "Why . . . er . . . why this sort of meeting?" she asked, still looking at him steadily. "Why not in my home?"

"I wanted to be private with you and I couldn't be sure your aunt or your cousin would allow that. They seem to look at me as though I were some devouring creature ready to strike."

She put up a brow quizzically. "And, of course, you are not?" By now he had led her to his coach and was helping her into it.

He took up the empty place beside her, stretching out his legs onto the worn upholstery before him and turning to smile at her. "Of course I am not," he answered easily and tapped for the driver to move on.

"Where are we going?" she asked immediately, for that voice was now hammering in her head.

"Just for a tour of the town," he said and pulled at the shade of her window so that they were hidden away from curious eyes.

"Why did you do that?" she asked, and this time some of her fear crept into her voice.

"Are you so suspicious of me? Do you really think I

would ravish you here and now?" he asked on a light note. "My dear Satin, I only mean to protect you from curious eyes. It wouldn't do for you to be seen alone with me in a closed carriage. Why give the tattlemongers meat to chew?"

Again he gave her logic that seemed flawless. She pushed herself into the corner of the coach and faced him, her gloved hands in her lap. "You said if I came this morning to meet you we could discuss our future. You said perhaps you wouldn't rush me into this marriage you say you want . . ."

"Indeed. However, there are certain stipulations, certain whims that you must agree to adhere to before we can compromise," he returned on a serious note. He was leaning forward, reaching into a picnic basket. "May I offer you some refreshment? Some wine, cheese . . ."

She shook her head. "No, I am not hungry."

"A little negus then. It is just the one you like so . . ." He wasn't waiting for an answer, but was carefully doling out a portion into a deep glass.

"No, thank you . . ." She found him putting the glass into her gloved hands.

"Go on, it will make all this so much more comfortable if we could relax," he said easily.

She was irritated by his overbearing manner, but she took up the glass and sipped the drink. Her throat was dry from the ride and so she took a longer draught after that, sat back farther against the squabs and sighed.

"That's it," he assuaged, "drink it down, and I'll put the glass away." He was himself sipping idly at his wine.

"What stipulations?" she asked, getting right to the point.

He laughed. "You don't mean to waste any time, do you?"

"My aunt and father will be wondering where I am if I don't get back soon, so we might as well get to the point." She finished off the negus and handed him the glass, watching him idly as he put it away.

"Right, then, the stipulations. I would require you to keep the Duke of Morland at arm's length. I would require you to accept me as a suitor and to try to find pleasure in my company." He was watching her intently now.

She eyed him for a moment. "Not—not see Wildfire . . ." How silly of her to speak thusly to him. What must she sound like? How nicely the carriage swayed, and the passing of scenery went undetected as she attempted to gaze out of the shaded window. Odd, she had this slow sense of easing coming over her . . .

"Wildfire, is it?" He pulled a face and released a derisive snort. "Indeed, then, you will not see him! I am appalled that it seems to distress you. How far has your relationship with the infamous *Wildfire* gone?"

"How far . . . ?" What was he asking? Why were his features blurring? "Oh . . . I don't know really . . . he is very special . . . isn't he?"

"Is he?" Sir Edward found himself growing irritated. "You will try and forget him, my dear. He wouldn't have you—at least not for a wife—so you are better off without him in your sphere, for he will end in breaking your heart. I will end, however, in fulfilling it."

"No," she said, shaking her head and feeling strangely woozy. "No . . . I don't love you . . . in fact, I am not even sure that I like you. How can I? Look what you would stoop to just to have your way. It isn't me you want, Ned . . . it is your way . . ."

He shook his head. "You are wrong. I want you, Satin. I have from the moment those mischievous dark eyes lit over some naughty prank you played and I was witness to it." He took up her gloved hand and held it. "Satin, I am a desperate man and so I am doing all this, out of love, out of my desperate love for you."

"Nonsense. You don't love me. You find me interesting and then I rejected you, so you must erase that rejection by forcing me to the altar—and your bed. If you loved me—really loved me—you would put me above you; You would care first about what *I* wanted . . ." She found herself yawning. "Oh . . . please excuse me . . . I don't know . . ." It suddenly dawned on her. The negus. Oh, faith! The negus. She opened her eyes wide for a moment. "Ned, what have you done?"

"I don't know what you mean," he said quietly, not meeting her eyes. He found himself wincing beneath her scrutiny. What seemed easy enough in the quiet of his room, in the heat of his plans, seemed cruel and devious beneath those large dark eyes.

"The negus?" Her whisper was filled with the terror of her shocking realization.

He held her hand still and patted it. "It will be fine, don't look so distressed, Satin."

"No . . . oh . . . what have you done?" She could scarcely keep her eyelids from drooping, but somehow she forced herself to remain upright, she forced herself to look at him. "Please, Ned, take me home. . . ." And then she knew that he wouldn't. She knew in that moment what he intended and her heart gave out. "Please . . ." On a sob she clutched at his hand.

He frowned deeply, for she had touched something inside of him he thought long dead. But he couldn't turn back now. Too much had been instigated. If it didn't end with her as his wife, he would look a fool. At least once they were married, there would be those who would excuse him, say he was a romantic taken by the fever of love's passion. Yes, the marriage would cleanse the deed.

He pulled her into his arms because she was too drugged to fight him off and held her to his chest, stroking her cheek, taking off her hat, playing with the dark curls at her ears. "Hush, Satin, it will be all right . . . I will make it so."

A blackness was enveloping her. She couldn't stop the dark stream from rushing at her, weighing her down. She couldn't put it off and even the tear that had formed and fallen from one bright dark eye couldn't move him from his purpose. Her last thought as she fell into the canyon and lost herself was of a man whose blue eyes touched her soul, but even her Wildfire couldn't help her now.

Chapter Twenty

"Damnation!" *Sir Charles* exclaimed as his horse tripped over a log and suddenly went onto three legs in an accentuated dipping movement. He jumped to the ground and went to his horse's hind leg, which was lifted off the ground. "What in thunder . . . there isn't a rock . . ."

"Walk him, Charles," the duke said on a serious note, his dark brows forming a frown and his blue eyes imperceptibly taking in their surroundings. They were still quite a distance from Brighton and some distance from any town.

Sir Charles took the reins over his horse's head and led him a short distance, but the poor animal hopped on three legs, afraid to put any weight down on his sore left hind one. "Good Lord!" Sir Charles looked at his animal. "He was fine just a few moments ago. He took a bad step over that fallen tree—and bang, off he went on to three. What's to do? I certainly will not get on his back, and damn if I know how far we are from town."

"Why don't you take up position here, Charles, and I'll ride to the first posting house and bring back a mount for you. Then you can pony walk him to the stable where we can give him the proper attention."

Sir Charles pulled at his lower lip. "I'm not sure, but as I recall, I think there was an inn of sorts at Lewes and we should be no more than six miles away." He sighed. "Right, then, you go ahead, and I'll keep walking. It will help to walk him anyway. . . ."

"Agreed," said the duke at once. "But if you are to walk, make sure you don't take any side trips, Chuck, for I don't want to be out looking for you with a horse in tow." The duke eyed him quizzically for this was unlikely (given Sir Charles's nature) and it was meant only for banter.

"Go to the devil!" Sir Charles returned sweetly.

"The sad truth is that I shall in the end, and these days I have the strongest urge to go elsewhere," the duke was grinning broadly.

"Aye. No doubt to the heaven of Lady Satin's arms?" The twinkle had returned to Sir Charles's eyes.

The duke laughed. "Amen, Chuck, ole boy, amen!" With that he turned his horse about and took off in a steady canter down the main pike.

Cory had not taken up a maid and she had not gone to the Brighton stables to take up any hired chaise. Sir Edward had taken too much for granted when he supposed that she would do these two things. Miss Bretton had a mind of her own and though she was not impulsive she rather thought she would ride her own horse to Lewes and make better time. It was therefore just shortly before twelve that she found herself hopping down from her sidesaddle, brushing the dust off her spencer, sticking her crop into her riding boot and looking around. The inn seemed respectable enough. It was an old, Tudor-styled building with a barn that looked larger than the main building. There were several chickens strolling about at leisure, and a fat, white goat eyed her suspiciously for a long moment.

"Nice goatie," said Cory, attending to immediate pressures first. "There . . ." she said soothingly as she walked by, her horse in hand.

A small stable lad came running out of the barn and hung his head.

"Sorry, mum, didn't hear ye . . . was out 'ere . . ."

"That's all right. Just walk him for a bit before you water him and stall him with a flake of hay, for I don't know how long I will be."

The boy agreed to do this "up proper" and took her horse off. This left Miss Bretton facing the main entrance of the inn. She took a long breath of air and went within. There was no sign of Sir Frederick, no sign of Satin and no sign of Sir Edward. She had this awful feeling that all was not right with the world. "Well, now," she said softly to herself, "a fine hem set out I have gotten myself into."

Sir Frederick saw the inn ahead and called to his driver to come to a stop before they pulled into the courtyard. For the hundredth time that morning he wished his arm was in better condition as he scanned his surroundings. Nothing seemed to be out of the way suspicious and with a shrug he signaled for his driver to proceed.

A moment later he was jumping out of his carriage and taking long, hurried strides to the inn's front door. It was just within that he found Miss Bretton questioning the innkeeper. She turned to him and breathed, "Thank goodness, Freddy, you are here." With that she dove into his arms, wrapped her own about his waist and laid her cheek against his chest. "Something is wrong—dreadfully wrong—and I can't fathom what."

"Cory, I don't understand." Sir Frederick wanted to comfort his love, but felt the situation needed some explaining.

She pulled away and eyed him. "You didn't write me that dratted note, did you?" Miss Bretton had very quickly surmised the matter.

"Note, what note?"

"No, of course you did not. But then how do *you* come to be here?"

"Why, you sent for me. I received a note that . . . Zounds! Tell me we have been made the butt of some joke?" He was astounded. "But why?"

"It isn't a joke, Freddy." Cory was attempting to think and pressed her gloved fingers to her forehead as she pulled away from the safety of Sir Frederick's hold.

"Not a joke? What, then? I don't understand. Where is Satin?"

"That is just it, Freddy. In the note"—she suddenly thrust her hand into the inside pocket of her riding skirt, then waved the note in front of his face—"you said she was here with Sir Edward."

He took it and read it, saying after a moment, "I can't believe this. Who would write such a thing to you in my name . . . ?"

"Sir Edward would!" returned Cory, her temper on the rise and her voice was not untouched by fear as well.

"Sir Edward would what?" It was a strong, male voice at their backs.

Cory turned and found the Duke of Morland filling the doorway. He was certainly an imposing figure, and she could see why a girl of Satin's stamp had fallen irretrievably in love with him. Something inside of her relaxed. Here was the duke—what did Satin always call him? *Wildfire.* Right, then. Here was Satin's Wildfire, and for some reason she believed he, if anyone, would straighten out this mess. "Thank goodness you are here," she answered him.

"Something awful has happened and, in truth, I am at a loss this time to set it to rights."

"I repeat," said the duke calmly, "Sir Edward would what?" He was sure this pertained to Satin and anything pertaining to Satin automatically drew his wholehearted attention.

Quickly, breathlessly, Cory advised him about the events of the morning. She summed it up by shoving her note into his hands, allowing him a moment to read it and then allowing Sir Frederick to relate the contents of the letter he had received.

The duke took only a moment to consider the situation before going into action. "Freddy, take a horse, by whatever means you have available to you, and fetch Sir Charles. His horse has gone lame some miles back. Then see Miss Bretton home." To her he said gently, "I rely on your good sense in this matter to see to it that your aunt is not distressed and Satin's father is kept at home until he should hear from me."

"Yes, yes, of course, but, your grace, what will you do? Where is Satin? What has Sir Edward done with her?"

"I think that he has abducted her and is off with her by now. It leaves me only one course: to find their direction and eventually catch up with them, at which time I will escort Lady Satin home."

"Yes, but, your grace . . . ?" breathed Cory on a frightened note. "What if it is too late? What if he has already forced her to marry him?"

The duke's face took on a grim expression, and his voice was clipped and hard. "Then Sir Edward's life is forfeit!"

Sir Frederick and Cory turned to one another, and Sir Frederick frowned. He had only been able to understand snatches of what was happening. "Cory, love, I do wish you would expand on what you have told me so that I might get a clearer picture of what we are facing."

"Yes, and so I shall, my dearest, but first things first. You have to go to Sir Charles with a horse, and I—I am going to order some tea and enough food to eat myself silly!"

Chapter Twenty-One

Sir Edward moved the window shade aside and gazed at the passing scene of sand and sea. There was the promise of sun in the variegated sky above, and the morning mist had dissipated with the warm summer breeze. He pushed the window jacket open and sighed. It was a lowering thought that he had come to such a pass. Here he was, abducting a lady of quality, one of his own class, because she wouldn't have him any other way! His ego was taking a beating.

What if she never forgave him this move? What if she never responded to him, to his lovemaking? It could make life a hell on earth. He turned and looked at her. He had set her on a pillow, but, even so, the bumping and lurching of the coach was going to give her some kink in her neck when she woke up. Just one more reason to despise him. He looked at the face in repose. She slept like a child, unaware, but she was aware, all too aware, of what he had done. And then he heard the driver of his coach howl with something close to terror just before the world closed in on him and his thoughts!

The duke rode hard towards Brighton. His horse was tired, and he was risking laming him, but the animal was also very fit and so he took the chance for, in truth, there was no time to lose and he knew it. He made the ten-mile journey to the resort town's center in just over an hour and called his groom curtly, ordering his horse to be seen to and another to be sent for as quickly as possible.

He took only a moment to run to his lodgings, then walked grimly, resolutely, across to his dark oak gun cabinet and withdrew his Manton horse pistol. This he stuffed into his black waistband before returning to his stables. All the while a picture of Sir Edward putting his hands on Satin stayed in his mind and caused him to grind his teeth. How could he bear it if Sir Edward touched her? He couldn't. There was only one answer to that, and he assuaged his jealousy with the thought of putting Ned underground.

As he strode hard round the bend of the avenue to the alley that housed his leased stable building, he encountered the count coming towards him.

"Ho there, Nicholas!" the count called for his attention.

"I haven't time, Otto—later," the duke answered roughly, without stopping.

"Yes, but, Nick, just a moment . . ." Otto hurried after him and fell into step. "It's about Satin . . ."

That had the power to stop him in his tracks. "What about Satin?" the duke asked sharply.

"That's just it," said Otto thoughtfully. "I thought seeing that Sir Edward was a friend of yours . . ."

"He is not. We are acquaintances, not friends," said the duke testily, "but do get to the point, Otto."

"I am. Give a man a chance!" snapped the count, taking affront. "I was riding on the beach this morning and saw Satin. I was just about to call to her when I noticed this hired coach drive up and out came Sir Edward. He handed Satin into the coach, tethered her horse at the back, and off they went." He frowned. "That isn't like Satin. She wouldn't go off with a man like Sir Edward—alone. She isn't cut like that. Went by her place and the household there is looking for her. All they know is that she said she was going for a ride on the beach. Don't like it."

Otto found his shoulders being clutched. "Which road did they take? Come on, man, which road?"

"Aye, I watched them for a time, and he turned off the main pike and took the sea route . . . the one that runs along the coast and through Hove."

"Good boy!" The duke was excited. He slapped the count across his arm and was off.

The count called after him, "Yes, but what does it mean? Damn it, Nick, where are you going? What is happening?" The duke was across the street and he wasn't bothering to answer. There wasn't time. There just wasn't time.

The driver of Sir Edward's hired coach saw the ditch in front of the horses, but it was just too late to do anything about it. The rut stretched across the main pike as though an angry saber had slashed through the heavens and divided the road in half. He made the attempt to pull in his team, cursing them for not seeing it themselves. The horses couldn't stop in time, though they tried to answer the hard yanking at their mouths. The driver slammed his hand against the lever braking the wheels as the horses jumped the wide, rutted gully. There was nothing to do but cry out a howling sound of terror and to shout to his passengers to hold tight for the front wheels were already diving and cracking into the gutted earth.

The driver was flung forward, the horses were yanked backwards and the carriage pitched deep into the wide ditch so that it nearly toppled over itself. Inside, Sir Edward was flung so hard that he hit his head against the wall before him and was for a space in time knocked momentarily unconscious. Satin's limpness was a blessing as she was thrown against the squabs in front of her and then she fell onto the floor. She groaned and seemed to come out of her sleep for a moment, winced with the pain of the bruises she had just received and slipped off again into sleep.

Sir Edward came to and found Satin's boots in his chest. He lay there attempting to compose himself and trying to understand what had happened, where he was and who he was. He heard the driver calling to him.

"Sir Edward . . . hey there, flash . . . Sir Edward, can ye 'ear me?" The driver was certainly hurt, but he had not been knocked out. Hurriedly, he scrambled to see to his passengers.

Ah, Sir Edward thought, that is who I am. He looked at Satin, who was now pushing unconsciously with her feet, digging the heels of her boots into his chest. He lifted her legs and put them aside. That's right, the thought process continued, I am Sir Edward, running off with Lady Satin. Right, so where am I?

"We landed in a ditch, sir. Road must have washed out in last week's rain," said the driver, answering the second of Sir Edward's silent questions.

"I am in a ditch," said Sir Edward out loud, for he was attempting to assimilate the situation and set things to rights. He sat up straighter and eased Satin into a better position. One of the coach doors was hanging open and swung on its broken hinges. He moved to it and gently eased himself out, turned, took Satin's hips and even more gently slid her slowly to him. The driver helped at this juncture and between them they had her out and on the wet grass.

"A blanket for the lady." Sir Edward was now getting hold of himself. There was a nasty gash across his forehead and it was bleeding down the side of his face. He brushed the blood away with the sleeve of his blue superfine, grimaced at the sight of blood staining his jacket and reached for the blanket the driver had retrieved from the inside of the carriage. This he laid on the ground and then lifted Satin onto it.

Her eyelids fluttered for a moment and she said on a low note, "Nick . . ." Then her lids closed again.

There was a nearby boulder and Sir Edward dropped onto its flat silver surface and sank his uncovered head into his hands. Things were not going exactly as planned.

The duke had lost his hat somewhere along the way and his ginger-colored hair blew about his head as he rode hard and fast. He took the coast road, his thoughts tumbling over one another. It was nearly two o'clock. If Ned had taken Satin up at noon, he would already be at Hove. Why Hove? What was there? It was the nearest coast village, but other than that, it had nothing to recommend it. Damn the man's eyes! How dare he treat Satin to such a display.

He was neatly planning to run the man through at the very least, when the overturned coach came into perfect view before him and he slowed his blowing horse. "What the deuce . . . ?" he breathed out loud and then caught sight of Satin stretched out on a blanket. "Hell and brimstone! I'll have the man's heart cut into pieces for this!" was what he breathed into the wind before urging his horse forward once again.

Satin stirred, and her eyelids fluttered open. She had been laid out in the fresh air for more than forty minutes now. Sir Edward was pacing, waiting for the driver, who had taken a horse and gone bareback into town to return with another carriage and some help. She saw Sir Edward moving to and fro. It was a hazy vision, and she tried to raise herself onto her elbows. "Where—where are we?" She was attempting to steady her aching head and found that she had to lie back down. Her hand went to her forehead in that flat position and she groaned.

Sir Edward went to her at once and took her hand away from her forehead and held it. "Satin, you are perfectly well. Don't try to move. We have had an accident. . . ."

She opened her eyes again and looked at him. "You drugged me," she accused, for all at once she remembered.

"Not now, Satin. We have a problem we must deal with first . . ." He was tired suddenly and not in the mood for a confrontation. The sound of horse's hooves brought his head up, and then all of a sudden there was Wildfire taking him up as though he were weightless and landing him a belly blow that doubled him in half. Before he had time to do more than groan painfully, he was dealt yet another blow to his jaw and reeled with the onslaught of this.

Satin was once again on her elbows and thinking that perhaps she was dreaming. It was an excellent dream and so she could not help but smile and call out, "Nick, oh, Nick, you are here."

He turned to go to her immediately, for he was ragged with fury and concern. She was deathly pale and so helpless-looking there on the grass, attempting in her valiant way to ignore her weakened condition. He scooped her up into his arms. She held on to him for dear life, resting her head on his shoulder, and sighed his name.

"Oh, Nick." She didn't seem to feel it necessary to elaborate and say more at that time.

"What is it, love? What has he done? Were you hurt?"

"He drugged me," she said, and then took his cheek in her hand to stop him from putting her down and going after Sir Edward again. "But never mind it now. Just take me home, please."

He kissed her forehead feverishly. "Beloved," he whispered in her ear, and then turning on Sir Edward, his charge still in his arms, he warned, "It has not ended here, sir."

Sir Edward pulled himself up and said with as much dignity as he could muster, "I am at your disposal, your grace, whenever you decide you want satisfaction in this matter. However, you have the prize. I concede the loss, suffice that as punishment enough for me and spare the lady's reputation."

It was true. He couldn't duel Sir Edward without Satin's name being in danger. While he hesitated, Satin asked, "Is my reputation safe then, or do you mean to call in your marker for this day's work, sir?"

Sir Edward eyed her for a long moment and said quietly, "I take it from the duke's action that he means to make you his wife. How could a duchess be considered anything but mysteriously, wonderfully eccentric when they find out she is also an authoress? What is forbidden to most, is always allowed in a wealthy duchess." He bowed himself off and went to walk some distance away.

The duke looked down at Satin and then hoisted her onto his grazing horse. "I suppose there is a reasonable explanation for that remark of his?"

"You suppose correctly, my Wildfire, but first, hop up behind me and keep me from falling." She waited until he had done this and had his arm tightly clasped round her waist before proceeding. "And answer me, was he right? Do you mean to wed me, or do you call all damsels in distress *beloved*?"

He laughed, mostly from relief at seeing her her old self.

"I mean to wed this damsel. Now you tell me: What did he mean?"

"Ah, kiss me, Wildfire, and seal the bargain." She cocked her head at him. "Then maybe I will tell you my big, dark secret."

And so it was, he did, and then she did. This left only the wedding, which took place in London in the fall. It was a lovely double ceremony, for Sir Frederick and Miss Bretton were also married. Sir Edward? He left on that very day in fact, and . . . well that is another story altogether!

Love...
Romance...
Passion...

CLAUDETTE WILLIAMS